IN A DIFFERENT LIGHT

GROWING UP IN A YUP'IK ESKIMO VILLAGE IN ALASKA

Other books by Carolyn Meyer

Nonfiction

The Mystery of the Ancient Maya

Fiction

Killing the Kudu

(Margaret K. McElderry Books)

IN A DIFFERENT LIGHT

GROWING UP IN A YUP'IK ESKIMO VILLAGE IN ALASKA

CAROLYN MEYER

◆ with research assistance by Bernadine Bainton ◆

◆ contemporary photographs by John McDonald ◆

◆ archival photographs courtesy of the University of Alaska Fairbanks ◆

McELDERRY BOOKS

MARGARET K. McELDERRY BOOKS
An imprint of Simon & Schuster Children's Publishing Division
1230 Avenue of the Americas
New York, NY 10020

Book design by Ann Bobco/Ed Miller
The text of this book was set in Garamond 3
Printed and bound in the United States of America
First Edition
10 9 8 7 6 5 4 3 2 1
Library of Congress Cataloging-in-Publication Data
Meyer, Carolyn.
In a different light: growing up in a Yup'ik Eskimo village in Alaska /
Carolyn Meyer with research assistance by Bernadine Bainton; contemporary
photographs by John McDonald.—1st ed.
p. cm.
Includes bibliographical references and index.
Summary: A study of the contemporary Yup'ik culture in an Alaskan
village as seen through the eyes of a typical family.
ISBN 0-689-80146-7 (hardcover)
1. Yupik Eskimos—Juvenile literature. [1. Eskimos—Alaska.]
I. McDonald, John, ill. II. Title.
E99.E7M547 1996
979.8'004971—dc20 95-31140
CIP
AC

Photographs on the following pages are courtesy of Archives, Alaska and Polar Regions Department, University of Alaska Fairbanks: p. 50, Geist Collection; pp. 57, 70, 78, Romig Collection; p. 76, Folger Collection; p. 84, VF Eskimo Children; p. 94, Holmes Collection; p. 101, Llano Collection; p. 152, Johnson Collection; p. 111, VF Eskimo Games.

All other photographs courtesy of John McDonald of Bethel, Alaska.

FOR JEAN GREENLAW

CONTENTS

Part I: Freeze-Up 1

Chapter 1: October 5
Chapter 2: November 19
Chapter 3: December 33
Chapter 4: January 47
Chapter 5: February 61
Chapter 6: March 74

Part 2: Breakup 89

Chapter 7: April 93
Chapter 8: May 107
Chapter 9: June 120
Chapter 10: July 132
Chapter 11: August 146
Chapter 12: September 159

Epilogue 173
Bibliography 175
Glossary 176
Index 177

PART 1
Freeze-Up

David Koonuk waits for snow. Hunting, fishing, and gathering are over until spring, and the whole village is ready for winter. Any day now snow will cover the tundra, and life in this Yup'ik Eskimo village on the southwest coast of Alaska will turn inward.

Frost slicks the boardwalk that connects the old school buildings on the east end with the airstrip and the new school on the west. By Egoak's store one branch of the boardwalk forks toward the church and the community center and the old houses by the river; the other passes the health clinic and the post office. At the airstrip the boardwalk swings sharply south, skirting the ponds, and runs through the new part of town known simply as Housing. Offshoots lead to the generator, out to the dump, to anyplace else you might want to go in

Chaputnguak, Alaska, population 361, home of David Koonuk, age thirteen, his sister Adeline, who is eleven, their brothers and sisters, parents and grandparents, uncles, aunts, cousins, and other relatives, which include many of the villagers.

Sunrise arrives later each morning, taking its own good, slow time. The sky turns golden, reflecting on the frozen mirrors of the ponds. In other parts of the United States it is autumn, but here in Alaska it's freeze-up, one of the major turning points of the year. The signs have been increasing for the past couple of weeks on the flat, watery tundra. The spongy ground is frozen hard, and the ice on the ponds is thick enough to drive across on a fat-tired four-wheeler. After the snow comes, the tundra will become a vast, unbroken expanse of frozen wasteland.

David's eighth-grade teacher has told them that every place on earth receives exactly the same amount of sunlight in the course of a year, but in the Far North the light comes in the summer, when for days the sun doesn't set, leaving the darkness for the long winter, when for weeks the sun barely creeps above the horizon. Instead of a twenty-four-hour turn of light and dark, the cycle lasts twelve months. At freeze-up the year is winding down toward a time of deep cold and long, long nights.

At the equator, the teacher says, the sun rises and sets on a line nearly straight up from the horizon, so that dawn and twilight are brief, while near the Arctic Circle they are long and slow. As winter approaches, the sun

Yup'ik Eskimo children play on the frozen pond
before snow covers it for the winter.

sinks late in the afternoon, painting the sky with vivid pinks and purples. During the night the wind howls down out of the north. Chaputnguak hasn't long to wait.

Chaputnguak is a fictitious village, but it is also a *real* one—real in the sense that this is what a coastal Yup'ik village in Alaska is like—part of the United States and yet isolated from it by geography and climate, by language and culture, and by history and experience. David and Adeline Koonuk and their relatives are a fictitious family, but it is a real one in that same way: this is how many Yup'iks of this remote area live, struggling to remain who they are and at the same time striving to find a place in harmony with the outside world.

CHAPTER 1

October

In the blue house, third from the end of the boardwalk, an alarm clock buzzes. It's still dark as midnight when David pulls on his jeans and T-shirt, splashes water on his face and hands from the basin in the kitchen, and brushes his teeth. He grabs his jacket and works his feet into his sneakers, and he's heading for the door when his mother stops him: "We're almost out of water."

David takes a couple of plastic jugs and trots down the boardwalk to a public watering point. These small red-painted sheds are spaced along the boardwalk, connected by thick white arctic pipe, water pipe buried inside a heavy foam jacket, that runs next to the boardwalk from the well at the opposite end of the village. Every time David complains about this chore, his father tells him about the Old Days—the 1970s, when Jim

Koonuk was growing up—when there was no pipeline and no pump, and Jim had to haul water jugs in a wheelbarrow from the well, a pipe sunk far below the frozen surface. He didn't have far to go then—Jim's family lived right across from the church in the old part. "Housing" didn't exist then, and neither did the public watering points or the sewage-collection system. Jim enjoys telling his kids how he used to carry the "honey bucket" full of excrement down to the river and dump it, letting the current carry the sewage out to the ocean a few miles away, or how in winter he just flung the sewage out on the ice, where it stayed frozen all winter until—*pheewwww!*—it melted during spring breakup. Now a tank towed by a four-wheeler makes the rounds through the village, collecting everybody's honey-bucket stuff and dumping it in the lagoon, out of sight—and smell—of the village.

David fills the two jugs and retraces his footsteps across the broken plywood that forms a crooked path to the house over the mud, now frozen. The house where David and his family live is pretty much the same as everybody else's in Housing, since they were all brought in on a barge at the same time in the early 1980s. The house perches on stilts a few feet above the ground, facing south, away from the prevailing winds and the snowdrifts that will soon pile high. Jim has finished nailing a temporary plywood skirt around the stilts, to keep the wind from blowing under the house and making it a little less drafty in winter. Bingo, the dog, likes it under the house, and until recently Jim's snow machine, covered with a plastic tarp, was parked there. For the past couple of weeks Jim has been tinkering with it, getting it ready to go as soon as the snow comes.

A wooden board with Jim Koonuk's name carved on it is nailed by the porch. There are other Koonuks in the village, of course: David's uncles, Pete and Andy and their families, and his grandfather Charlie, and Charlie's brother Wally, and Wally's son Jack, and some others not so closely related. Some of them live in Housing, some in the old part.

The half dozen steps up to the house are slick with frost. The enclosed porch is cluttered with heavy winter gear and Jim's outboard motor, plus a couple of birds that David and his cousin Judson shot. Later his mother will make them into soup. She has taped a sign on the door, TAKE OFF YOUR SHOES, so there is a pile of boots and sneakers near the door and an even bigger pile of coats and jackets. Next to that is a pile of tundra grass that his mother has gathered for stringing up next summer's herring catch.

Inside the house, a lumpy couch with worn upholstery is pushed against a wall full of family photographs. Next to it is a recliner chair that the kids sit in until their dad gets home. The television is hooked up to the village satellite dish, and they sometimes rent videos at Egoak's store, but they've all seen these pictures too often: they've watched *Jurassic Park* at least six times, maybe more.

The kitchen at the end of the living room looks like the kitchens on TV—electric stove and refrigerator, cabinets, and counters—except there is no sink. The house has a "bathroom" but no bathtub; the sink has no running water, and there is no toilet, just a honey bucket—a five-gallon can fitted with a toilet seat. A basin of water, soap, and a towel are kept in the kitchen. David often takes a shower at school after he's been playing basketball, and he goes to his uncle Pete's steam bath whenever he's invited.

David's parents, Jim and Lucy, have the largest of the four bedrooms. Two-year-old Lilly sleeps there with them. Adeline shares one of the other bedrooms with Katie, seven, and Agnes, eight; David sleeps on the floor in a sleeping bag next to Tommy, four, and Dennis, ten. But David has his eye on the little room off the kitchen, which is now occupied by his older brother Judson, whom his parents adopted when Judson's father died in a hunting accident and his mother, Lucy's sister, remarried and moved to Bethel. Judson will graduate from high school in the spring, and then maybe he'll go off to college. And David will move into that room. Maybe.

David dumps the water he's brought into the plastic storage drum and hurries out again, Adeline right behind him. His mother shoos the younger kids, calling to them in Yup'ik and then in English, "Time for school, let's go!"

Adeline stays on the boardwalk with the younger kids, but David shortcuts across the pond toward the old part of the village. The pond has been frozen solid for a couple of weeks now, and he's looking forward to skating when school's out. Now David has to stop at Carl and Anna's place—Anna is his dad's sister—and get his cousin Billy up and drag him off to school. Once he has coaxed Billy out of bed, David waits restlessly for him to

Many older homes like this one have been replaced by better insulated units.

get ready. This little house is completely different from his own. Cold and drafty now, before winter even begins, the plywood house is one of the oldest houses in the village, put up by the state of Alaska in the 1960s to replace the old sod houses. The place is a mess. The sticky linoleum is worn all the way through to the bare wood, dirty dishes are stacked in the sink, there are open cans and boxes of food everywhere, the bed in the corner is unmade. Anna's fat, spoiled little dog, Rippie, curls up on a pile of soiled laundry on the floor. Anna is still asleep; Carl is nowhere in sight.

Billy has slept in his clothes, so at least David doesn't have to wait for him to dress. David urges him on, hurrying now because if they don't get there soon, breakfast at the school kitchen will be over, and it's a long time until lunch. David's father Jim, the school's cook, has been in the school kitchen since seven, setting out cold cereal and reconstituted milk and canned fruit.

Up the boardwalk they race, sometimes losing their footing on the frosty surface, sometimes having to jump off altogether when a four-wheeler barrels past them. Everybody who can afford it has one of these all-terrain vehicles with four fat tires, but the fanciest in the village belongs to Walter Prescott, the principal of the school, and his wife, Marcia, and that's the one that passes them now. If Walter and Marcia are on their way to school, it means breakfast is almost over, too late for snap-crackle-pop but maybe still in time for peanut butter and pilot bread, a hard, round cracker.

It's starting to snow. The wind flings stinging crystals in their faces, and David and Billy duck their chins into their parkas and make a dash for the school, yellow and welcoming and glowing with light at the edge of the world.

Urrsukvaaq School, named for the river that flows past the village, hovers like a futuristic spacecraft above the vast blanket of moss and grasses and low-growing plants that freezes brick-hard in the winter and thaws in summer to mushy sponge. Under this foot-thick cover lies permanently frozen subsoil and rock, the permafrost.

The snow will bury the tundra throughout the winter—about five feet of it will fall—but the frequent "whiteouts" that keep planes from flying and snow machines from traveling and sometimes villagers from walking from house to house are not always fresh snowfalls but ground blizzards, rearranging the snow already on the ground. Sixty inches of snow and a lot of summer rainfall surprisingly add up to only about eighteen inches a year of precipitation in what is described as a semiarid region.

From the air the Urrsukvaaq River seems part of an intricate web spun of hundreds of small rivers and streams, lakes and ponds. To the north, the mighty Yukon River flows 1,900 miles from its headwaters in Canada. Miles south of Chaputnguak the smaller, slower Kuskokwim River meanders to the Bering Sea past dozens of Yup'ik villages. At one point the two rivers come within twenty-five miles of each other. Then the Yukon veers northward, the Kuskokwim turns south, and for the last two hundred miles of their journey to the sea, the two rivers form a great fan-shaped delta, an area the size of Kansas. The Yukon-Kuskokwim Delta is home to about twenty thousand Yup'ik Eskimos who live in some fifty small villages. Chaputnguak is one of those villages, located three airmiles from the sea, fourteen miles by boat, eighty miles from the nearest paved roads in Bethel. Chaputnguak is closer to Russia than to Anchorage, the largest city in Alaska, five hundred miles to the east. New York City seems as distant as the moon.

David has heard his grandfather tell about the time they moved the village. Years ago the village was at another place along the river, but every spring after breakup the floodwaters rose and turned the village into an island. The village elders—Grandfather Charlie's own grandfather, Qilangak, was one of them—wanted to have a school that would educate their children in the ways of the *kass'aq,* the white man. Finally they agreed on a new place where a school could be built. Gradually the village began to grow.

Even after that school was built, though, students who wanted to go to high school had to leave the village and go away to boarding school. After a court decision in the 1970s, any village that wanted its own high school could have one, built by the state of Alaska. David remembers when the new Urrsukvaaq School was put up a few years ago, materials and equipment brought in by barge, much the same way as the school in Qilangak's day.

Building on the permafrost is like building on frozen mud; that's why the village houses sit up on stilts. A foundation sunk into the soil, the kind used in the Lower Forty-eight, does not work; it melts the permafrost and eventually sinks in, and the building on it warps and twists. Instead, the school is set on pilings filled with refrigerant and sunk deep into the frozen mud, an extremely expensive way to build.

The preschoolers still use part of the old school at the other end of the village, but 110 students, first-graders through high school seniors, attend Urrsukvaaq, among the most up-to-date in the United States, with a computer for every three or four students and hair dryers in the shower rooms.

Painted on the outside of the building is the school emblem, a Yup'ik hunter in a fur parka poised to hurl a harpoon at his quarry, the way Qilangak once did. But the history of Chaputnguak reaches back much further than the lifetime of Qilangak—all the way back to the arrival of the first ancestors on this continent.

Thousands of years ago a bridge of land connected the continents of North America and Asia and separated the Bering Sea from the Arctic Ocean. As the level of the Bering Sea has risen and fallen throughout earth's history, this land bridge has submerged and emerged, building up a lush vegetation that lured animals such as the caribou from the pastures of Siberia to the continent of North

America. The nomadic hunters of East Asia followed the animals across the bridge.

Anthropologists believe that both Eskimos and American Indians trace their ancestry to East Asia but arrived at different times. The Indians, who probably migrated about twenty-five thousand years ago, spread east across Canada and south throughout what is now the United States.

The ancestors of the people who made their home in the farthest north and who were later called Eskimos (not an Eskimo word but an Indian word meaning "eaters of raw flesh") arrived on the coast of western Alaska some four to six thousand years ago. These more recent immigrants had physical characteristics markedly different from the earlier group: light yellowish skin, short, broad noses, and almond-shaped eyes narrowed by the fold of skin that covers the inner corner of the eye.

One group separated from the rest and spread throughout the Aleutian Islands, where they eventually evolved their own language and culture, distinct from but related to other Eskimo groups. The rest traveled eastward across Canada and into Greenland. Among the first were the Dorsets, who reached northern Newfoundland. Later came the Thules (pronounced THOO-lees), who invented the dogsled. This allowed them to travel more freely, and by about A.D. 1000 the Thules and their descendants inhabited the entire coast of the American Arctic, the ancestors of today's Inuits of Canada and

Inupiats of northern Alaska. The ancestors of the Yup'ik Eskimos, who have lived on the coast of the Bering Sea for about two thousand years, were among the last of the migrations. The terms Inuit, Inupiat, and Yup'ik all mean "the real people," and that is what these three distinct groups call themselves today.

Always during these ancient times there were bloody clashes between the Eskimos and the North American Indians. Eventually peace was established when the Eskimo groups adapted to life along the coast, leaving the wooded interior to the Indians.

When early explorers from Europe first discovered the Inuits of northern Canada who lived in igloos, dressed in fur, and hunted polar bears, these "snowhouse Eskimos" were actually only a few of the thousands of Eskimos then in existence. But they came to symbolize what people thought of when they thought of Eskimos—and sometimes still do.

Before Eskimo culture was overwhelmed by Western civilization, families moved their homes several times a year, following the fish, sea mammals, and caribou. The Yup'iks along the Bering Sea coast paddled their kayaks out into the sea to hunt for seal and whale and followed the broad Kuskokwim River and its tributaries, setting up fish camps and then moving on when the food supply moved.

It was Russians from the west, not European explorers and settlers from the east, who were the first to reach

Alaska. Czar Peter the Great hired a Danish sea captain, Vitus Bering, to explore far northeastern Siberia. In 1728 Bering set out from Siberia on his first mission and sailed through the narrow strait that separates the two continents. In 1741, Bering visited Alaska's southeastern panhandle, now known simply as Southeastern. Unfortunately, the ship was wrecked and Bering died on an island in the sea that was named for him. Survivors returned to Russia with news of the discovery—and with a collection of sea otter skins that triggered a "fur rush" of Russian traders to the Aleutians. The traders took what territory they wanted and exchanged trinkets for a wealth of furs. Terrible stories have been told of Russian treatment of the native peoples. Whole populations of some of the Aleutian Islands were wiped out.

The first permanent settlement of whites in Alaska was established on Kodiak Island, southwest of what is now Anchorage, in 1784. In 1799 Aleksandr Baranov, managing agent of a fur-trading enterprise on Kodiak, established Sitka as the first capital on Kodiak, one of the group of islands that is part of Southeastern. But Sitka did not thrive, and gradually Russian interests in Alaska began to decline. The Russians did leave one linguistic legacy: the traders called themselves "Cossacks," which became *kass'aq* (pronounced GUSS-uk) in Yup'ik and now means "white person."

Finally in 1867 Russia sold Alaska to the United States, which bought it at the urging of Secretary of State

Russians were the first white people to reach Alaska. Russian Orthodox missionaries later settled along the Upper Kuskokwim.

William H. Seward for $7.2 million. People called it "Seward's Folly," and at first no one knew what to do with this enormous piece of property equivalent to one-fifth the land area of the continental United States. When gold was discovered around Juneau in 1880, a governor was finally appointed, and in the early 1900s the capital was moved to Juneau. Alaska became the forty-ninth state in 1959.

If most people saw little use for this cold, isolated land, Christian missionaries recognized it at once as an area greatly in need of their efforts. They began to arrive in the late 1870s. Soon there were dozens of missions scattered through the territory. The Moravian church took over the area of the lower Kuskokwim River, and the Russian Orthodox church went upriver. The Roman Catholics established themselves in certain isolated villages near the coast—including Chaputnguak. The missionaries had a big influence on the Yup'iks, but so did the *kass'aq* schoolteachers who came after them, and the health care workers and government employees.

Then television began to beam the whole wide, complicated outside world into Chaputnguak and other remote villages by satellite. And since then life among the Yup'iks has never been the same.

CHAPTER 2

November

On the wall by the window a computer-generated banner declares COOPERATION MAKES OUR ROOM GREAT! Beneath it the teacher, Catherine Tom, has mounted her students' photographs and their names, eight fifth-graders displayed on a green background, eight sixth-graders on red. Adeline Koonuk's picture is with the red group. Her brother Dennis is green.

The girls have been playing jacks in the corner, but now Catherine calls them to their seats, four rows of four individual desks, and checks attendance, entering it on a computer hooked up to the principal's office. As usual, a couple of people are absent, or maybe just late. She writes a sentence on the board: *them boys will substitute for jim and i on our ball team.*

"All right, let's work together at correcting this sentence. Does anyone see anything wrong?" They are an enthusiastic group, and Catherine has to caution them,

"Don't raise your hand unless you know the answer," but after a few false starts they figure out the punctuation and correct the grammar: *Those boys will substitute for Jim and me on our ball team.* The next few examples go smoothly.

Next there is the class science experiment to check: a jar full of sugar water with a string dangling in it has been sitting on top of a cabinet for a week. Adeline reaches for the jar. "It evaporated!" she announces. "We got crystals!"

Adeline's friend Libby has prepared a presentation for show-and-tell: a picture postcard of a polar bear in the Anchorage Zoo, sent by a cousin who went to the city on a visit. The students listen attentively to Libby's description of the bear—there are no bears in this part of Alaska—and then Catherine asks for their comments.

"She should talk slower," Adeline suggests. Catherine smiles at Libby. "It was okay if you're talking to a New Yorker, but this is Chaputnguak." Everyone laughs. Most of the children learned Yup'ik first; English is a second language they speak well, often switching back and forth.

Adeline loves Catherine, a young Yup'ik Eskimo teacher from the village of Aniak, upriver above Bethel. Catherine got her teaching degree at the University of Alaska in Fairbanks, and last year returned to the bush—rural Alaska—to teach. Catherine and Monica Charles, who teaches first and second grades, are the only Native Alaskan certified teachers in the Chaputnguak school;

the rest of the "certs" all are *kass'aqs*—whites. There are several aides from the village; some are trying to become certified, but it means leaving the village to study, and that's hard to manage.

Adeline remembers when she first entered the preschool at the other end of the village, in the old building where her dad and mom went to school when they were kids. Everything was so different then, to hear

Children make their way to school through a snowstorm, tied together to prevent their getting lost in case of a "white-out."

them tell it. That old school went only to the eighth grade. Then, if you wanted to go to high school, you had to go to the regional high school in Bethel and live in the student dormitory or else go all the way to a boarding school like Mt. Edgecumbe in Sitka. Either way, you were gone all through the fall and winter and spring, coming back only for Christmas break. Adeline's dad talks about sneaking home from Bethel for seal hunting in the spring. Adeline's mother, Lucy, attended Mt. Edgecumbe for a year, but she got homesick and dropped out, like a lot of other students.

Now Catherine moves on to math, a mix of simple arithmetic, basic algebra, and a little basic geometry. The first row to get all the math problems correct earns the privilege of being first in the lunch line. Adeline's row is declared today's winner, and Adeline is chosen to head up the lunch line.

Adeline leads her group down the hall, decorated with cutout Thanksgiving turkeys. The group is quiet and orderly, because Yup'ik children are brought up to be quiet and orderly, and they file past the library and the computer lab and the audiovisual lab, past the high school classrooms, to the gym, where a half dozen tables have been folded down from the walls. Jim Koonuk stands behind a pass-through counter, filling plates.

Adeline usually knows what they're going to have for lunch: the school district office in Bethel sends the menus to her father at the beginning of the year, when the supplies are shipped in by barge, and a couple of times he has let her come into the pantry to look at the boxes and boxes of food, the enormous cans of vegetables, the giant jars of peanut butter, the freezers stocked with ground meat.

Jim learned at a job-training school how to make all kinds of lunches, mainly from hamburger meat and ground turkey. When he mixes the meat with macaroni and tomatoes, it's called goulash; substitute beans for macaroni and it's chili; meat and tomato sauce on a bun becomes a sloppy joe. Sometimes there are fish nuggets, tasteless fish that has been breaded and fried and frozen somewhere in the Lower Forty-eight. Jim heats it up and serves it with ketchup for dipping. This fish doesn't taste anything like the fish Adeline and everybody else in the village fish for in the river, or the herring her uncles catch in nets, or the salmon that swim into their fish traps. Fish makes up the main diet in Chaputnguak, served in all kinds of ways that the menu writers in Bethel never seem to think of: raw and dipped in seal oil, or dried, or boiled into soup, or buried and fermented underground.

On Thanksgiving the whole community will gather in the school gym for a special dinner. Adeline's father will begin days in advance to prepare the food that has arrived by air: frozen turkeys, packaged stuffing, canned cranberry sauce, and pumpkin pies—plus the traditional feast food, *akutaq,* shortening whipped with sugar and berries. Called "Eskimo ice cream" by the *kass'aqs,* it was traditionally made by grating tallow, the hard white fat of reindeer or caribou, and beating the tallow with seal oil to form a soft, smooth fat, like shortening—so much like shortening, in fact, that most women now use Crisco instead, which is always available in the village store, while reindeer and caribou are scarce in this part of Alaska. Lucy and her sisters will help prepare the dinner, mixing the *akutaq* in large stainless steel basins, adding frozen salmonberries and blueberries with sugar and canned milk and instant mashed potatoes. In the Old Days, Jim tells his children, Thanksgiving was celebrated at home, with a swan or a crane prepared Yup'ik style—boiled, with rice and onions.

Adeline picks up a tray of food and sits down with her friends, Libby and Rose. Before they take a bite, the girls fold their hands and say grace, making the sign of the cross. There is only one church in Chaputnguak—Catholic—and everybody in the village is Catholic.

Adeline is pleased to see that no ground meat is masquerading today as something else; instead there are baked chicken legs, instant rice, canned green beans, bread, and canned pineapple. The bread is the best thing; Jim learned to bake bread in cook's school, and Adeline can tell by the taste that he made this himself. There is also something different: a tray of raw baby carrots and broccoli and a bowl of ranch dressing. Rose turns up her nose: "It would taste better with seal oil," she says, scraping off the dip.

By the time they've finished, the seventh- and eighth-graders are lining up. Adeline, Libby, and Rose find a corner of the gym and spend the rest of the half-hour lunch period playing jacks.

After lunch Catherine produces a macramé kit for each student—a length of string and instructions for making something called a sailor's bracelet. The instructions are complicated—even the teacher has trouble. It seems they each need a plastic bottle around which to form the bracelet and nobody has a plastic bottle, but Rose gets a bright idea: she will make her bracelet around Adeline's wrist, and then Adeline will make hers around Rose's—if they ever figure out the instructions. Just before frustration wins out, arts-and-crafts period is over.

The fifth-graders head for the computer lab, where one of the *kass'aq* teachers will work on keyboard skills, and the sixth-graders troop off to the library. Adeline's favorite class is reading, and the library aide has labeled her a "bookworm." Adeline is excited about the Battle of the Books, a nationwide competition for kids from third through eighth grade. Last year her class won for the district, and they're determined to repeat their success. On her list this year are *Number the Stars,* by Lois Lowry, and *Roll of Thunder, Hear My Cry,* by Mildred Taylor. Her favorite book is *Bridge to Tarabithia,* by Katherine

Paterson; it makes her cry, even though the world described in it is like nothing she has ever seen.

David's teacher, Jerry Waterman, a tall, lanky *kass'aq* with thinning hair and a droopy mustache, is very well organized, and he's trying to teach his seventh- and eighth-grade students to be organized, too. "When you go Outside to the Lower Forty-eight," he tells them, "you have to get things done *on time,* be where you're supposed to be *on time."* So he has posted the class schedule on the board: 8:45 language arts, 9:30 reading group, 10:00 journal writing, 10:15 PE, on and on. And he sticks to it, too.

Jerry gets annoyed when somebody comes late to class, although it happens every day. Another thing that gets to him is when students ask to go to the bathroom, right in the middle of his explanation of a lesson. "You have to learn to control that," he tells them. "You're old enough." But nothing seems to improve.

The first class after lunch is social studies and geography. Jerry divides the class into groups of four, each with a world globe. David struggles to remember the difference between the revolution of the earth around the sun and the rotation of the earth on its axis, and his team loses points on that one when he mixes them up, but his team pulls ahead when David correctly identifies latitude and longitude.

From this they move into a lesson on agricultural

societies, how people got the seeds they needed for planting, and what "domesticated" means. "How many of you have ever planted a seed and watched it grow?" They did once, in first grade, David remembers; a bean, maybe. A green shoot came up from the dirt, but nothing much happened, and then it died.

Jerry lays aside his textbook and gives them a little lecture. "Historically," he says, "hunters and gatherers were nomadic people who have been replaced by farmers, people who stay put in one place and grow their food. Like where I'm from in Nebraska. But your dads go seal hunting and fishing, and your mothers and grandmothers gather berries and greens from the tundra, right? So," he continues, "the Yup'iks are still hunters and gatherers—maybe one of the last hunting and gathering societies on earth!"

At the mention of seal hunting David allows himself to drift a little, dreaming of the time he'll be allowed to go with his father and uncles, maybe late next spring. And then his mind does a little skip, and he wonders what it would be like to live on a farm. He's seen pictures in books, and the animals look interesting—he's never seen a horse or a cow, for instance, except in books—but the idea of putting seeds into the ground and taking care of the plants and then cutting them or however you harvest them, that doesn't sound like much of a life. He'd rather fish and hunt seals any day.

The minute school is dismissed, Jerry and some of the

high school boys grab their sleeping bags and duffels that they've brought to school and head for the airstrip. The boys' basketball team, the Hunters, is flying to Shnamute for a game, and half the school assembles to see them off.

Basketball is almost an obsession in these isolated villages, and the Chaputnguak team has been a district winner quite a few times. During PE this morning, David's class immediately split into teams, boys against girls. Jerry, who coaches the Hunters, has been showing the girls how to play more aggressively. They're small and quick, and they manage to keep the ball out of reach of the boys, although once the boys get hold of it, they're better on the long shots.

The Twin Otter, a two-engine propeller plane that flies a regular route among villages in the bush, touches down on the gravel strip. Mail, freight, and passengers come off, and ten minutes later the Otter is in the air again with the team on board. They'll stay overnight, spreading their sleeping bags on the gym floor. David isn't old enough for the team, but he shoots hoops every evening from eight-thirty until ten o'clock in the school gym and on the outdoor deck until midnight or later in summer.

Judson is on the team, one of the Hunters' star players, and he's been talking all week about the trip to Shnamute. Judson talks about going to college next year, maybe even trying for a basketball scholarship. David has noticed that no Yup'iks play on the big college and

Basketball, a sport that can be played indoors year-round, is practically an obsession in isolated villages.

professional basketball teams, but the reason is obvious: Yup'iks are short and compact—"close to the tundra," their coach Jerry says—nowhere close to six feet, let alone seven, like the big stars.

But Judson is ambitious, and he'll figure out another way to go to college. David thinks that four years sounds like a long time to be away from the village. He knows lots of kids who said they wanted to go, but then they got homesick and came home and eventually dropped out. Nevertheless, Walter Prescott, the school principal, is very proud of his students. Since he came to Urrsukvaaq School ten years ago, more than fifty kids have finished high school, and at present four of them have either graduated from college or are still attending. There's a good chance that Judson will make it five.

Adeline is torn. School is out, but she can't make up her mind what to do: go hooking—fishing through the ice—for tomcod, or attend cheerleading practice.

Judson's girlfriend, Alice Beans, who moved to Chaputnguak from Bethel two years ago to live with her grandparents, has formed a cheerleading class which meets after school. Alice is rather unusual for this village: she knows hardly any Yup'ik, and she complains sometimes about missing life in Bethel, about not having plumbing. Like a *kass'aq,* Adeline thinks. But Adeline decides to hang around her class and watch.

Alice lines up her pupils in the gym and starts

teaching them the words and the moves. Her big worry, she has confided to Judson, is that when the girls get in front of a crowd of people, even if it's their own relatives from the village, they'll be too shy to jump and yell like real cheerleaders. It turns out that the beginning cheerleaders want to go hooking, too, and they urge Alice to cut short the practice and come with them. At least, Adeline thinks, Alice knows how to do *that.*

In the fall, when the ice first begins to form, the kids check the ice daily. When it's four inches thick, the word is out, and nearly everybody in the village goes ice fishing. In some places, ice fishing—also called hooking or jigging—lasts all through the winter. Here near the Bering Sea coast the season lasts only through October and November, when the fish—mostly tomcod and smelt and some ugly devilfish—are running upstream. On the way to the river Adeline sees her eight-year-old sister Agnes and her ten-year-old brother Dennis lugging sacks of fish. They've been lucky in their hooking.

There are still a lot of people on the ice. Some of the old women have been there all day. With a tarp thrown over a tipped-over sled to protect themselves from the wind, a box of food, and a little camp stove for making tea, they squat or sit on stools by the holes in the ice, about the size of a basketball hoop, dangling a stick decorated with feathers or the stems of certain plants. Some don't even bother with a hook. The tomcod is a stupid fish and will snap at anything that attracts its attention. When the fish go for the lure, the women scoop the fish out of the water with a net—four or five at a time—and onto the ice, where they soon freeze. They catch hundreds of fish that way. Some of them will be stored in the fish house, some fried or boiled. Dennis tells Adeline that pretty soon the ice will be too thick to cut through, maybe in the next couple of days, and the fish will be gone.

Adeline finds that Libby and Rose have already caught a pile of fish—they keep their hooks in their school lockers and stop at the river on the way home from school. Adeline forgot hers, but she does have the piece of tangled string from her macramé project. She settles down with her friends and starts hooking for supper.

Later that evening Adeline sits on the floor, playing Monopoly with Libby and Rose and Dennis, who is winning big-time. Then the news comes on the CB from Shnamute that the Chaputnguak Hunters have trounced their opponents, 57–35. The girls abandon Dennis, who now owns a number of hotels and utilities, and Adeline teaches them the cheer she learned this afternoon. The girls yell and jump just the way Alice would want them to:

Bang bang, choo-choo train!
Come on Hunters, spell your name!
H-U-N-T-E-R-S, Yea!

CHAPTER 3

December

Snow lies thick on the frozen tundra, nights are long, and the sun creeps above the horizon for only a short time before it sinks again. It is bitterly cold. The wind howls out of the northwest, and the windchill factor hovers at thirty degrees below zero, a temperature at which exposed flesh freezes quickly. Most people stay inside.

But on a Saturday before Christmas the wind subsides, and David and his father go out to check the mink traps. A few weeks earlier they buried some cone-shaped traps near the river—the same traps they used for catching blackfish—to catch the animals that feed in the water under the ice. Mink skins, dark and glossy with a little white patch at the throat, are the most valuable, but sometimes muskrat and otter get caught, too.

Fur has traditionally been one of the chief sources of cash for Yup'ik families. For a while the animal rights activists in the Lower Forty-eight caused a big slump in the market, but Japanese fur buyers have more than made up for that. Jim's job doesn't leave him much time for trapping, but he likes to tell David about when Grandfather Charlie was considered one of the best trappers in the village. The Koonuk family once had extensive trap lines—not a "line" at all but an area recognized by other families and passed down from father to son. Charlie was often away for days at a time, traveling far from the village to check on his traps. Pete and Andy have taken over most of the traps, but Jim still keeps a few close to the village—they can always use the extra cash.

Lucy is just as happy if they don't catch anything, because it's her job to skin out the animals, a dirty and unpleasant chore. But when David carries in three good-sized animals, she goes to work: with each mink she cuts away the sac under the mink's tail that produces the acrid smell, cleans the skin, turns it inside out with a board inserted, and hangs it up to dry. She boils some of the meat for supper and stores the rest in the village freezer.

A few days later Judson borrows Jim's snow machine to go riding with his friends and comes home with an arctic fox tied on the back. He tells them how he spotted it, even though it was now turned pure white and nearly invisible against the ice and snow, and chased it down, running it back and forth until it dropped. Judson reached it first and hit it over the head with a hammer. The pelt will fetch good money from the dealer in Bethel.

A couple of years ago a musk ox showed up in the

Fox pelts drying in the winter air will be sold to a trader in Bethel. Fur is still an important source of income for Yup'ik families.

village. There is a herd on Nunivak Island, far off shore, but nobody had ever seen one of the shaggy beasts around here. There was no time to ponder how or why—every man in the village ran for his gun. David's great-uncle Wally dropped the animal with one shot. He divided up the meat among the village families and nailed the woolly hide to the wall of his house. The skull with its down-curving horns stares across the pond.

Cash is always short in Chaputnguak. The best time of year is late fall, when the Alaska Permanent Fund checks arrive. In the 1970s, when oil started flowing through the pipeline from the Arctic North Slope, the state legislature began funneling oil money into a special fund. Once a year the fund mails a dividend check of eight hundred dollars or more to every man, woman, and child in Alaska—thousands of dollars for a large family. Lucy's uncle, Ted Egoak, and her cousin Larry make sure their store is well stocked when the checks are due. The four-wheeler that Jim Koonuk bought last spring for five thousand dollars on a handshake will be paid off now, other debts will be settled, and a new round of buying will begin.

There are few paying jobs in the village. The school is the biggest employer. The federal government pays the postmistress and health care workers. Two VPSOs—village public safety officers, the local lawmen—work for the state police. Lucy Koonuk clerks in her uncle's store.

David's aunt Anna earns a little money calling numbers for the afternoon bingo games, sponsored by the village council. The problem is that Anna also plays, and she ends up spending everything she earns, and then some. Three afternoons a week, from one o'clock until five, about fifty women and a half dozen men crowd the floor of the community center, each with a dozen or so faded bingo cards and a bag of plastic markers. Between rounds, Anna's sister-in-law sells candy bars and soft drinks. She also sells "Rippies" for two dollars apiece, pull-tab cards with flaps that are ripped open in the hope of finding three-of-a-kind symbols: three tiny bowls of soup, for instance, pays three hundred dollars. Customers buy Rippies by the fistful. An afternoon of bingo and Rippies may cost a player a hundred dollars or even more. It's a lot of money, but Anna looks at it another way: sometimes she wins. Besides, the money stays in the village—it's used to pay the men who take care of the electrical generator and the water system, and Anna's husband, Carl, who collects the honey-bucket waste. There are no local taxes, and bingo is a way of financing village operation.

On bingo days Adeline's mother takes time off from the store to run over to the community hall. Lucy tries not to spend too much, and this is a chance to visit with friends. It's good for business, too—the players come by the store when they're done to pick up something for supper, and if they've had a lucky day they might even buy one of the high-ticket items, like the three-hundred-dollar bread machine. Lucy has been thinking of buying it herself, as a Christmas present for Jim.

Adeline stops by the store after school to visit her mother. She likes to look at the shelves stocked with *kass'aq* food, cake mixes and dried soup and canned vegetables, the freezer filled with pizza and fried chicken and ice-cream bars, and the cooler with milk and fruit juice. Twice a month a shipment of food comes in by plane—apples, oranges, loaves of white bread, and Adeline's favorite, Twinkies. There are also disposable diapers and detergent, T-shirts and tools, brooms and buckets, and a rack of rental videos. Egoak's is a lot like the big stores in Bethel, but a fraction of the size.

Larry's younger sister Pauline works in the store, too, but she's bored to tears—she wants to get out of Chaputnguak. Pauline graduated from high school last spring, and she talks a lot about moving to Bethel and getting a job clerking in the big AC store or Swanson's. The summer before her senior year, Pauline enrolled in a program designed to give high school students on-the-job experience. For one precious month she lived in a dorm in Bethel and worked at the AC. Ever since, she's been dreaming of going back, but so far it hasn't worked out: the job she wanted went to somebody else.

Adeline tries to be helpful. "But wouldn't you get lonely?" Adeline wonders, and then Pauline has to admit, "Probably. But I'd come home to visit. I wouldn't miss Christmas."

A few days before Christmas everyone has gathered in the school gymnasium for a program put on by the schoolchildren, capped by a visit from Santa and the annual gift exchange.

Each room has rehearsed a special presentation. David's room performs "The Twelve Days of Christmas," with local variations: "eight seals a-swimming, seven huskies running, six cans of Pepsi," and then David's line, "a five gal-lon juuuug," which gets a laugh from the audience every time he stands up and waves a water jug. Last on the program are Monica's first- and second-graders, who present a manger scene with a real baby and lots of shepherds and angels. They sing "Away in a Manger" in Yup'ik and then, joined by the community, in English.

The serious part over, Santa makes his entrance.

Around the middle of October Walter, the school principal, started letting his gray beard grow out full and bushy. Now, two days before Christmas, he dresses up in a suit of long red underwear and a red baseball cap and makes his entrance in an old dogsled towed by eight high school boys while the girls shake strings of bells and sing "Here Comes Santa Claus."

Santa and some volunteer helpers have a big job ahead of them tonight, distributing the mountain of gifts stacked at one end of the gym. Nearly every family in the village exchanges presents at Christmas, and eventually each family has accumulated a mound of packages. With a burst of "ho ho ho's" Santa is towed out again, and pretty soon Walter is back, in his usual plaid flannel shirt, smiling broadly. There are some people in the village who think that the honor of being the one who gives out the gifts should go to one of the village elders, or maybe to one of the important men on the village council, like Ted Egoak. But Walter seems to enjoy doing it so much; it would hurt his feelings, and they like Walter, they think he does a good job with the school, and so they say nothing. Maybe if Walter leaves this job, somebody else will take over as Santa—one of the local people, not a *kass'aq.*

Soon the gymnasium is filled with a welter of wrapping paper, ribbons, and boxes. Adeline gets a Polaroid camera and some packages of film and an album in which to put her pictures. She wishes she had had the camera when Walter was dressed in his red suit, but she'll have to wait for next year.

David is thrilled to receive a pair of cross-country skis. There are few slopes for skiing on the flat tundra, but sometime this winter Jerry will take the boys by snow machine to the low hill that bulges up from the tundra a few miles from town and let them slide down on pieces of plastic. David means to take his skis along, after he's had time to practice on the snowdrifts banked against the houses.

Judson has been given a fine new gun. He hopes to get his first seal this spring, and he's certain this gun will bring him luck. Dennis is happy with his tape player and several new video games, and Tommy has a bike that he'll be trying out long before the snow disappears from the boardwalk. Katie clutches a blue-eyed blond-haired Barbie doll. Her grandmother, Liz Koonuk, has made the Barbie a *qaspeq,* a flowered cotton parka cover, to match the ones she made for each of her young granddaughters.

And then there are presents to and from all the relatives. Grandmothers have knitted caps for the children, men have bought ammunition and tools for brothers and cousins, women have wrapped sheets and towels and kitchen equipment for one another. Everyone has been careful not to leave anyone out and not to give gifts that might seem stingy. A lot of money has been spent, and now everybody has more stuff to find a place for.

Jim Koonuk takes his place behind the pass-through window, serving the pizzas that were flown in frozen from Bethel, paid for by the village council. Then the party is over, and each family loads its hoard of new possessions into the sled behind the snow machine and heads for home.

On Christmas Eve the entire village turns out again, this time for midnight mass at St. Cecilia's, squeezing into the small church built twenty-five years ago when the population of the village was half its present size. Father Frank McGuire, a *kass'aq* sent from Fairbanks, serves four villages and spends one week a month in Chaputnguak. The rest of the time one of the deacons—often David's great-uncle Wally—conducts Sunday and weekday services. The parishioners are pleased that Father Frank is at St. Cecilia's for Christmas this year, even though that means he won't be here for Easter.

Dennis is an altar boy, and David is the crucifer, both dressed in white cottas, customary in the Catholic church. People wear their best clothes for this occasion—Liz put on the necklace and earrings Jim gave her for

Christmas—but it's so cold in the church that they stay bundled in their heavy jackets. Then the Kiyutelluk family arrives. Martha Kiyutelluk is the acknowledged expert in skin sewing in the village, and every one of her children and grandchildren wears a sealskin parka trimmed with a wolverine ruff around the face, and beautiful beaded sealskin boots.

The little electric organ cranks out "Oh Little Town of Bethlehem," and a handful of women sitting nearby sing the carol in Yup'ik, harmonizing in two parts. When Father Frank gives the nod, Dennis starts down the narrow aisle carrying a lighted candle, followed by David, holding the wooden cross aloft.

The service progresses slowly as everything that Father Frank says is translated into Yup'ik. Babies cry, toddlers whine, and parents constantly move in and out to tend to the restless children. At last Father Frank tells them to go in peace, and the procession moves up the aisle while the women sing another carol.

On the way home David looks up at the black velvet sky just as the northern lights begin a sacred dance across the heavens.

Two days before the end of the year, when the weather promises to stay clear, Jim tinkers some more with his snow machine, gasses up, and hooks the home-made wooden sled to the back of it for Lucy and the girls. They're going to Shnamute for a visit while the school is closed, an annual occurrence that has been planned for weeks. Judson has managed to borrow his uncle Larry's snow machine. Larry parts with it only after an unnecessary reminder that it's brand-new and cost a lot of money. Judson loves to drive it, certainly the most powerful machine in the village. Tommy and Dennis ride in the sled behind it; David straddles the seat behind Judson.

They have dressed in their warmest parkas, but it's still a cold, rough ride. Lucy pulls a tarp over the children to protect them from the wind. Several other Koonuks and Egoaks are making this trip, and soon a caravan is strung out over the tundra, following tripods of sticks that mark the trail to the next village. In some ways this is the easiest time of year to travel—at least they can go in a straight line. When the snow is gone, the roundabout trip by boat takes much longer. The trail is in good condition, and in a little over an hour David, peering over Judson's shoulder, can make out the cluster of dots that is Shnamute. The caravan sweeps across the frozen pond and into the village, scattering in different directions among the homes of relatives.

The Shnamute families greet them warmly and put the teakettle on to boil. The adults settle down to talk. Dennis immediately gets involved in a Monopoly game with some of his cousins. Adeline uses some of her precious film taking photographs of her friends. David shows off his new skis by skimming down some of the drifts and landing in a heap at the bottom. Judson cruises slowly through the village, imagining that his uncle's fancy snow machine belongs to him.

That night they eat in whatever house they happen to be stopping and sleep wherever there is space. The plan was to stay for a couple of days and see in the new year, but the next morning Jim rounds them up; the weather is changing, and he's anxious to start for home. If a major winter storm moves in, they could be in Shnamute for days. Judson recalls a year ago when he and the basketball team were stranded for over a week, sleeping on the floor of the school gym, while a storm raged and no planes flew. Knowing how fast everything can change, they stay close together.

Then something happens: the fan belt snaps on Jim's Polaris, and although people usually carry an extra, Judson—whose job it was—had apparently forgotten to replace the spare after the last breakdown. While they try to make do with an extra belt from one of the other machines, the storm strikes. One minute the sky is a somber gray, but visibility is good; the next minute the visibility drops to zero as a ground blizzard engulfs them. They have gone too far to turn back, and Jim makes the decision: it's too dangerous to go on. The rule is that if something happens, stay put. Quickly they pull the wooden sleds together, turn them on their sides, and take shelter behind them, huddled under the tarps. Anyone who wanders even a few feet away could lose his sense of direction and become hopelessly lost.

While they wait, David thinks about Mr. Ivanoff, one of the elders. Mr. Ivanoff is fond of saying that it is not really so much work to catch enough fish to feed a dog team. He reminisces about the time he was lost in a storm and the dogs could not find the trail. They burrowed into the snow together. The storm went on and on, and he had grown very hungry but the dogs kept him warm. Eventually the old man and his dogs were rescued. Sled dogs did not break down, he says. If the "iron dog" breaks down on the trail, it will not keep you warm. David thinks of Mr. Ivanoff's stories as he gets colder and hungrier.

For hours the wind howls and snow swirls around them, and then it dies down as suddenly as it came up.

Few Yup'iks still rely on dogsleds, preferring the convenience of snow machines, but the elders claim that dogs never break down on the trail.

David sticks his head out and peers around. Everything looks different; the trail has disappeared. The men emerge and study the situation. They locate the top of one tripod, and then another. Then, out of the darkness, they see dots of light approaching from the direction of Chaputnguak. Several men, alerted by CB from Shnamute that the travelers were somewhere in the storm, have come looking for them. The enlarged caravan starts off again, the bright cones of light from their single headlamps pointing the way toward home.

CHAPTER 4

January

Dennis, Adeline, and David are sprawled on the floor around the Monopoly set when the door opens and their uncle Pete stomps in, accompanied by a blast of cold air. He has walked only a few yards from his own house, but his parka is covered with snow crystals. He sits down at the table, and Lucy pours him a cup of tea and offers some pilot bread. The adults talk for a while, and then Pete eases into one of his stories. The Monopoly players lose interest in their game; Judson drifts in from his room to listen. Lucy gets up and switches off the bright overhead light. Pete is the storyteller in the family, and they all enjoy his visits, even though they have heard his tales many times before.

"At the time of this story," Pete begins, "there was an old woman who lived alone and was always hungry because there was no one to hunt for her, and the people in the village never brought her food." He speaks softly, his voice rising and falling. His listeners follow his gestures, his expression, his dramatic pauses, and they quickly fall under his spell.

In the same village lived two brothers, successful young hunters, Pete tells them, and the old woman decided to marry one of them. She washed her face, fixed her hair, put on her best parka, and went to the boys' home with her proposal: if one of them would marry her, she would cook for him. When one of the boys asked his father's permission, the older man refused, asking why he wanted to marry a woman old enough to be his mother. That angered the old woman. She made a statue of a bear and sent the bear's spirit to kill the father. Just before he died, the father told his sons to take his body to the old woman's home, along with a bow and arrow. The next day the old woman was found dead, an arrow through her heart.

The teakettle sings, and Lucy makes more tea as Pete begins another story, this one about a man who found a creature that was half worm and half woman with a beauty dot between her eyes. He took her home with him, and as he cared for her she gradually became less and less an ugly worm and more and more an attractive woman. But one day while he was out hunting, another man came and shot her with an arrow through the beauty dot.

Heartbroken, her protector moved away to another place.

Adeline sighs; this story always makes her sad.

Storytelling is important in Yup'ik culture, partly because it's a good way to pass a long winter night. But it is also a way to pass along the people's history and their legends. Some stories deal with ideas of right and wrong, and some are about how the universe came to be, like this creation story:

In the beginning, in the time before time, Raven beat his wings so vigorously that the darkness formed into a solid mass. With his talons Raven scratched the surface of the earth and carved out the Kuskokwim and other rivers and streams and mounded up the low hills along the edge of the tundra. Then Raven took stone from those hills and fashioned a man, but this stone man sank into the wet tundra. So Raven took earth and created a man, and the earth man survived and thrived on the riches of the sea and the land and the air. His descendants are the Yup'iks, the Real People.

After Uncle Pete leaves and the family goes to bed, David curls up in his sleeping bag and thinks about the stories. He knows that long ago, when people often had several husbands and wives in a lifetime, men sometimes married women much older than themselves who were experienced in preparing meat and making skin clothing. He doesn't doubt that the spirit of the bear killed the boy's father, but a worm turning into a woman? Well, who can say it didn't happen that way, David decides, and he drifts off to sleep.

Life was much different in that long-ago time, David has been told. People didn't live in houses like his family's. At one time every village in this part of Alaska had a *qasgiq,* a men's communal house made of sod, built partly underground, where the men and boys of the village lived and worked together. Their wives and daughters lived in separate little sod houses and prepared food to bring to the men in the *qasgiq.* The old men trained the boys, teaching them to make tools and to

Before the influence of white missionaries, Yup'ik men and boys lived in large communal houses built of sod, women and girls in smaller sod houses.

build kayaks and traps for catching fish and small animals. The boys listened to the old men's stories, and they took sweat baths together.

Sometimes the women and girls came to the *qasgiq* for meetings and for dancing and storytelling. In summer parents and children moved to fish camp together, and in fall the families moved again to hunting camp. But in winter everyone returned to the village, the men to live in the communal house, the women in their separate homes.

A few of the elders still remember the traditional *qasgiq.* Mr. Kiyutelluk, now the oldest man in the village, helped to build one when he was a boy. The first job was to excavate a pit. Then the men and boys collected logs that had drifted down the river. They set upright posts at each corner of the pit and arranged a grid of logs across them to support the roof. The women and children gathered grasses, which were woven into mats laid over the logs to keep loose dirt from sifting through. The men packed thick blocks of sod over the structure, and the women topped that with moss. Soon grass and weeds began to grow on the earth covering, helping to hold it together.

In the middle of the *qasgiq* was a pit where an open fire was built for a fire bath, which was the traditional way of bathing. A hole in the roof above it let in light and let out smoke. The winter entrance led from a porch through an underground tunnel. In the fall the women brought in dry grass for the floor and the beds and placed braided grass all around the inside walls. The men slept on skins, and they lit and heated the sod houses with seal oil lamps.

But then the U.S. government entered the picture, replacing the snug sod houses with flimsy, hard-to-heat plywood dwellings. The sod houses slowly melted back into the earth and disappeared.

The modern community center with glass windows and vinyl-covered floors is a good place for bingo and dinners, but not for steam baths, introduced by the Russians, which replaced the traditional fire baths. Many families in the village have built their own small bathhouses, crude wooden shacks heated by a fifty-five-gallon fuel drum turned on its side, fitted with a stovepipe, and fueled with whatever is available: driftwood, old rubber tracks from snow machines, rags soaked in oil. And they call this bathhouse a *qasgiq.*

"Want to take a steam?" Jim asks one evening, and David says yes.

There is room for only four people in the shack. David's father and uncles use the steam bath first, and then David and his cousins take their turn; the women will have their steam later. The boys stoop to enter the outer room, too low for standing upright. Lined with soggy cardboard, it is cold and damp. They hang their clothes on nails and crawl on hands and knees through a little door into the steam room, illuminated only by the glowing fire. Their fathers had added more fuel before they left, and the tiny room is very hot.

David sits on the wooden floor while his cousin Brian ladles water over the layer of hot rocks on the flattened top of the drum. The water hisses and steam rises in scalding clouds. David breathes shallowly to avoid taking the steam into his lungs. In seconds he begins to sweat.

When the steam begins to subside, Brian throws more water on the stones. Suddenly the boys can bear it no longer and crawl hastily to the outer room. They sit on the low bench until they have cooled down. Twice more they steam; the last time they wash with soap and warm water dipped from a bucket next to the fire. They dress and amble back to the cousins' house, not feeling the cold.

"Want to play Nintendo?" Brian asks, and they slide effortlessly into the late twentieth century.

Aunt Mary's baby girl is being baptized Sunday morning, on Father Frank's next visit to St. Cecilia's, and Adeline gets to sit up front. The baby is being given three names—Inaq'aq, the Yup'ik name for her great-grandmother who died a few weeks before the baby was born; Theresa as her baptismal name; and Denise, because her mother likes it.

Before the arrival of the traders and missionaries, a Yup'ik baby was given just one name. But the whites insisted that each person must have both a Christian name and a family name. It took a long while for the family names to be sorted out; each *kass'aq* seemed to have a different idea of how it should be done. As a result, the rows of mailboxes in the village post office carry a mixture of names, some distinctly Yup'ik, some Russian, some *kass'aq,* and some derived from *kass'aq* given names, like Billy and Joe. But babies still receive Yup'ik names as well as others. Qetunraq, for example, means simply "son." Panik, a common name for girls, means "daughter." Most names can be give to both boys and girls.

When the first Christian missionaries arrived in Alaska late in the nineteenth century, they divided the Yup'ik villages of the delta among the three main church groups—the Moravians claimed those around Bethel and the lower Kuskokwim, the Russian Orthodox went upriver, and the Roman Catholics struck out along the coast—and set about converting the Yup'iks to Christianity. That meant trying to stamp out shamanism—the spirit world that Uncle Pete describes in his stories.

But traces of the old, pre-Christian religion still exist. The custom of giving Denise the Yup'ik name of a relative who died recently is not just a way to honor the dead; Yup'iks believe that the spirit, the soul, of the one who died must be passed on to a newborn. The Yup'ik word for soul is *yua,* which translated into English is "its person."

Before the arrival of Christian missionaries, Yup'iks and other Eskimos did not make a distinction between the natural world and the supernatural world of spirits. They believed that animals, like people, had souls. If the animal's soul was not pleased with the hunter and his people, the animal in which the soul dwelled would not allow itself to be killed. The Yup'iks also believed in reincarnation among animals; the *yua* of the dead seal retreated into its bladder, and the bladders were kept until they could be honored at a religious festival and pushed through a hole in the ice so the *yua* could be reborn in another seal.

Because their survival depended not only on their skill as hunters but also on having plenty of game, the Yup'iks observed a number of rituals and taboos to be sure there would be enough animals to kill. One way to please the animal's spirit was to treat the animal with respect; a dying seal was offered a drink of water, and its throat was cut to release its soul, its *yua*.

Sometimes when game animals were scarce, people believed that someone had broken one of the rules and that the spirits were angry. They would try to make amends to the offended spirits, usually under the direction of a shaman. Before the coming of Christianity, the shaman was a powerful person in the village. He claimed to have contact with the spirit world, and his people believed he had the power to protect them. Not all shamans were forces for good, however. There are stories of shamans who became dangerous and met violent ends. But whether good or evil, shamans were extremely influential.

The missionaries tried to eliminate shamanism and to substitute Christianity in its place. What often happened, though, was that Christianity became an addition, rather than a substitution—God the Father, Son, and Holy Ghost were just more spirits that had to be pleased.

Unaware of any of this, little Inaq'aq/Theresa/Denise wails as Father Frank pours baptismal water over her head, and her family smiles at her fondly, content that the spirit of Great-grandmother Inaq'aq is settled at last in its new bodily home.

It is time to get ready for the potlatch, the biggest social event of the year. Guests are coming from Shnamute to enjoy the traditional Eskimo dancing that is prohibited in Moravian villages—along with gambling, drinking, card playing, and *kass'aq*-style dancing. There is the usual concern about the weather, which has been typically stormy with relentless, howling winds, but on the last Friday in January the howl suddenly drops to a whisper. By late morning the sky is bright, and by noon a dozen snow machines with sleds have arrived. Guests are also expected from villages to the north, but the distance is much greater, an arduous trip of four or five hours by snow machine, and most of them will fly down. Yup'ik rules of etiquette say that visitors may sleep or eat wherever they wish without prior invitation, returning the hospitality when visitors come to their village. And nobody ever knocks before entering.

Yup'ik women have always enjoyed dressing in their finest fur parkas for special occasions.

Late in the afternoon everyone gets dressed up. Lucy has a parka made of fox fur trimmed with bands of inlaid calfskin and decorated around the sleeves and hem with beadwork and mink tassels. Jim's mother made it for her years ago, and she preserves it for special occasions like this one. Everyone else in the family wears the new clothes they got for Christmas.

Meanwhile Jim carries some smoked salmon and

frozen whitefish from his family's cache in the community freezer to the school gymnasium as his contribution to the potlatch dinner; for once he's not the cook. He makes a second trip with a carton of canned fruits, pilot bread, tea bags, and sugar. Tonight the women are dancing, and by custom the men prepare the food. After dinner they clean up, and everyone finds a place to sit on the floor.

Lucy and her mother and a dozen other women, carrying dance fans made of grass coils interwoven with neck hairs of reindeer, congregate in the hall. Not all the women dance—only those few who particularly enjoy it. Five men sit cross-legged with their drums—their only musical instrument, a piece of ripstop nylon tent fabric replacing the traditional walrus gut stretched taut over a two-foot circular driftwood drum. They begin to drum softly with a thin willow wand.

During the dinner the women were given new nicknames for the occasion by the drummers. Now one of the drummers calls one of the women by her nickname and demands a gift from her. The woman brings candy or tobacco and presents it to the drummer. Then she dances while the men sing. She keeps both feet on the floor as she sways, bending her knees, gracefully moving her arms and hands. Each song tells a little story. Some of the songs and dances are very old; others have been composed for the occasion. When she has finished her dance, she joins the rest of the audience and another woman is called.

After the dancing is over—it goes on for hours—the women carry in armloads of gifts that have been stashed in another room. Then, starting with the oldest, Mr. Kiyutelluk, the men pick out what they want from the mountain of gifts. Round and round they go, until the heap of gifts is gone. Jim gets a new camp stove; Judson finds ammunition for his rifle; David chooses a pair of ski goggles.

It's long after midnight when the first potlatch ends, but the next evening they start all over again. This time the women prepare the food for the men, and the women sing the songs and call the nicknames of the male dancers. The men's fans are wooden, decorated with chicken feathers dotted with black ink to imitate snowy owl feathers, and they perform sitting back on their heels. When the dancing ends, the gift selecting begins, leading off with the oldest woman, David's great-grandmother Amelia. Lucy picks a teapot and matching cups; Adeline acquires a leather purse; Katie gets fancy socks.

On Sunday morning, after only a few short hours of sleep, David and his family attend mass. Before the Moravian relatives leave for Shnamute, they invite the Chaputnguak people to the rally to be held in their church. Since Eskimo singing is taboo in the Moravian church, the music will be strictly Protestant hymns. Although Chaputnguak is a Catholic village, probably two-thirds of the people will make the trip south for the two-day songfest. The point is to visit friends and relatives and to enjoy more feasting, although there will be no gift exchange. In a couple of weeks the Koonuks will head south again, following the trail of crossed sticks.

And so the winter passes. Planes come and go on a schedule dictated by the weather. Supplies of frozen, smoked, or preserved food gradually dwindle, but Egoak does a brisk business in *kass'aq* food. Except in the most extreme weather, the children play outdoors, sliding on the snowdrifts and playing a version of baseball on the frozen pond. The women play bingo and work on their baskets. The men tinker with their snow machines and begin to think about seal hunting. The wheel of the year turns slowly toward spring.

CHAPTER 5

February

Katie hangs back shyly among the first- and second-graders trooping off to the health clinic with their teacher. Somebody discovered head lice among the children, and the health aides, Nancy and Marie, begin a search for the tiny white nits that cling to the children's thick dark hair. The kids, waiting their turn, regard it as an adventure. The health aides separate the children into two lines, those with lice and those without. Katie is relieved—no lice on her head; but her friend Tina is given a little bottle of medicinal shampoo. She is sent home to have her mother wash her hair with it before she comes back to school.

Nancy and Marie both graduated a few years ago from the Urrsukvaaq High School and then went to Bethel for intensive training in community health care and trauma and other emergency treatment. Routine health care in the bush villages depends on the health aides at the clinic. They dispense common medicines, like antibiotics and pain relievers. They give regular checkups to pregnant women, before it's time to send them to the prematernal home in Bethel to await the birth of their babies. Most babies are born at the Public Health Hospital in Bethel, because it's safer. Then the aides take care of the new babies when they come home.

Nancy says the most important instrument at the clinic is the telephone. There are no doctors in any of the villages, and when something comes up that the aides are not trained to deal with, they phone the doctor at the hospital in Bethel. But there are only fourteen doctors at the hospital; each one is assigned four or five villages and is responsible for an average of twelve hundred patients—far more than the national standard of eight hundred patients. Twice a year the doctor flies out to the village, staying for several days each time, and gives everyone a thorough checkup. A public health nurse comes through every few months. Specialists make quick trips, like the pediatric cardiologist who treats Agnes's baby sister, Lilly, born with a hole in her heart. Dentists visit once a year to deal with tooth decay, a common problem—maybe because of the high sugar content of the *kass'aq* diet the Yup'ik people have adopted.

Sooner or later everybody visits the village health clinic, where the aides consult with doctors at the hospital in Bethel by telephone.

Emergencies are serious. If the weather is good and Bethel has a plane available, it takes an hour for the plane to reach the village to pick up the patient and another hour to fly back. But coastal weather is changeable, and sometimes days go by before a plane can get in. When David broke his arm skating a couple of years ago, the plane didn't come for three days, and his grandmother tied a piece of red yarn near the break to prevent infection.

By the time David and his mother arrived at the big, strange-looking hospital—everybody calls it "the Yellow Submarine"—he was too scared and in too much pain to care what the *kass'aq* doctor would say about his grandmother's traditional remedy. But the emergency room doctor just snipped off the yarn, talking to him gently the whole time. She might not have been so unconcerned if she knew that his grandfather routinely treats frostbite and all kinds of minor cuts and sores with urine, *teq'uq,* and sometimes it was drunk to reduce a high fever. Teq'uq is the Yup'iks' old standby for healing.

Not all stories end as well as David's. People remember the boy who was badly injured in a snowmobile accident during a winter storm. The health aides did what little they could, and everyone prayed, but there were no planes for a week, and the boy died before the weather lifted.

Yup'ik Eskimos are especially vulnerable to respiratory diseases, like tuberculosis, influenza, and pneumonia, all introduced by white men who made the first contact with the Native Alaskans. Russian traders brought tuberculosis; in the 1880s one of every three Yup'iks died of TB. Those who survived were sometimes too weak to hunt and starved to death. The rate of TB among Native Alaskans was estimated at twenty times the rate for the rest of the United States. In the 1950s the U.S. Public Health Service began treating TB with chemotherapy, and the number of deaths dropped. Now everyone is tested regularly, and tuberculosis is no longer feared as it once was.

Gold prospectors spread other deadly epidemics: influenza and measles killed nearly half the Yup'iks along the Kuskokwim River in 1900. After that came whooping cough. In Goodnews Bay, some distance south of Chaputnguak, every child in the village died of whooping cough in 1940. Only forty-eight people were left alive, and for thirteen years there was no school in Goodnews Bay, because there were no children.

The honey-bucket system gets the blame for a lot of health problems. Septic tanks can't be used in areas where underground water is close to the surface. Untreated sewage lets germs spread. There is no running water for drinking and washing; water comes from wells or is hauled from nearby lakes or caught as rainwater, and this water is often contaminated. And many villages are located in low, marshy areas that flood in the spring, sweeping in refuse and vermin.

As some diseases become better controlled, other health problems get worse. Alcohol abuse is a modern-day plague. The accident rate in rural Alaska, mostly from drowning or snow-machine accidents, is four times as high as the rest of the United States. Most of these accidents are alcohol-related. Last spring Judson's best friend drowned while he was out fishing, and another friend suffered permanent brain damage when he got drunk and started acting stupid and wrecked his father's snow machine. Many people take their own lives while drunk.

It's all too much for some health aides, who look for something else to do that isn't so stressful. David has heard his parents talking about Nancy, who is a cousin of his father's. She says she can't take it anymore; she's thinking of training to be a school cook. At least in the kitchen it's not a matter of life and death.

David sighs, but he doesn't protest: his mother is sending him to check on Anna and Carl and to bring Billy over for supper. David dreads this. They're both likely to be drunk, because Carl has just made a trip into Bethel to visit the bootlegger, and he's brought home a few bottles of vodka. Having liquor always means getting drunk. Anna gets drunk right along with him.

Anna and Carl are not the only alcohol abusers in the village; they're just the ones David knows best. His mother's cousin Larry used to drink, but he's sobered up, or so he says. David's two uncles, Pete and Andy, are on and off the wagon, depending. There are plenty of others.

As if that weren't bad enough, there are the effects on the children. Billy has FAS, fetal alcohol syndrome, the result of Anna's drinking while she was pregnant with him. Billy has been placed in a special class with other learning-disabled kids, but he's a hard one to handle. David is one of the few people who seems able to deal with Billy, to get him up and dressed and out to school in time. One of the others is the special education teacher, Angela, who sits on the floor with her little class of sometimes outrageously behaving children, turns out the lights, switches on a flashlight, and whispers to them until they are calm.

Alcoholism is probably the leading health problem in bush Alaska. Yup'iks are binge drinkers, rather than steady drinkers. There is no such thing as "social drinking"—having a cocktail or two before a meal or during the evening. Alcohol is not always available, and when someone like Carl does get hold of a bottle, he drinks his liquor straight, either until the bottle is empty, or until he passes out. Once he begins to drink, there is no stopping him. And now that Anna drinks, too, there's no stopping her, either.

Carl used to promise Anna that he wouldn't drink anymore, but whenever somebody brought a bottle Carl was not able to resist the pressure. He'd tell his friends that he had decided not to drink. But they knew Anna had made him promise, and they would tease Carl, saying his wife was the boss. So Carl would start drinking again. It was a question of manhood.

The village council has tried to control drinking. No liquor is sold in the village, but people always seem to find a way to bring it in. For a while, a bottle or a case could be ordered from Anchorage and sent out by plane until that, too, was outlawed. Although it's legal to *have* liquor in Bethel, it's not legal to *sell* it. This doesn't stop the bootleggers, who make huge profits, clearing at least $350 on a case of whiskey. Since almost everyone from even the most remote villages where drinking is strictly forbidden comes to Bethel once in a while—to go to the doctor, to shop, to visit relatives—bootleggers make it easy to pick up a few bottles to take home.

In an effort to put a stop to that, a "search house" was built near the Chaputnguak airstrip, and for a while everybody flying into the village was taken from the plane directly to that shack and searched for any kind of alcohol. But eventually that procedure was abandoned, and now the old "search house" is abandoned, too.

There are other laws on the village books: appearing drunk in public in Chaputnguak can mean arrest by the VPSO and a fine; according to the law, fourth offenders are asked to leave town. But it doesn't always work that way; some people pay "third-offense" fines over and over. It's such a tiny place that villagers don't like to press charges and embarrass someone.

Often both parents are drinkers, like Anna and Carl, and then the children are neglected, left alone for days while the parents are on a binge. Sometimes the husbands and wives fight physically, and sometimes the children are beaten, too. No one knows how many children suffer from fetal alcohol syndrome; the rate of FAS among Native Alaskans may be the highest in the world. And no one wants to talk about any of this.

Before the arrival of white people, the Yup'iks had no intoxicating liquors, and they did not have the stress of living in two cultures. Traditional Yup'iks were people who had learned to live in balance with the most hostile environment on earth. But modern Yup'iks see themselves mainly in relation to Western culture, and in their own eyes they always fall short. Drinking helps them forget how bad they feel about themselves and how much they resent their increasing dependence on someone else's culture. Yup'iks are taught to hide their anger. But when they drink, the inhibitions disappear, and the pent-up anger erupts. Drinking lets them deny responsibility: "I didn't know what I was doing."

The drinking begins early, often in high school. Everyone worries about the effects of alcohol and drugs on young people, and the school does what it can to combat the problem. Urrsukvaaq School has declared zero tolerance for drugs and alcohol. In Dennis's third- and fourth-grade classroom there are posters featuring a clever-looking cartoon fox: "Too much of anything is no good," the fox advises. "Young people become chemically dependent faster than adults do." And, "Any alcohol for children is no good."

The fox may convince younger kids, but as they get older they may get caught up in a destructive cycle: drinking, fighting, sobering up, apologizing or shrugging it off, and waiting for the next chance to drink. Most of the violent crimes committed by Native Alaskans are related to alcohol. Self-respect dwindles, and the binges come oftener. Nothing seems to matter anymore. The spiral winds downward. Often it ends in accidental death—or in suicide.

The rate at which people take their own lives is many times higher in Alaska than in the Lower Forty-eight. Most suicides are boys and young men, who almost always shoot themselves. Life seems easier for a young woman, who has motherhood to look forward to and maybe even a part-time job. The young man trains for a blue-collar job, but then he finds there aren't any such jobs available in the village. Whatever work he gets is seasonal. Without money he can't afford the snow machine or the boat he needs to hunt and fish. He's not sure just who he is in this life, and it seems he has nothing to look forward to. Except the next bottle of whiskey.

Dennis notices the new sign above the drinking fountain in the gym: THIS IS NOT FOR SPITTING TOBACCO

OR JUICE, put there no doubt at the principal's orders, but there's a small brown quid of tobacco in the drain. The school secretary has her eye on him, so Dennis heads for the rest room to spit his mouthful of tobacco juice and saliva into the sink.

Like most of the children in the village, Dennis has been dipping snuff since he was very small. Even his younger sisters, Katie and Agnes, keep a pinch under their lips. Most of the adults use a mixture of chewing tobacco and the ashes of low-growing willows that the old women collect and burn.

Walter and Marcia, the *kass'aq* principal and his wife, have been on a campaign to stamp out "chew." First they put up a poster on the main bulletin board in the school entryway, featuring before-and-after pictures of a once-handsome boy now badly disfigured by cancer of the mouth, the effects of "chew." The poster hasn't accomplished a thing: Cancer is what happens to other people, like the boy in the poster, Dennis believes. His great-grandmother has been using snuff for years, and look at her!

There are posters everywhere in the school, always warning them about something—about how chew can give you cancer, about how drugs can mess you up, about how alcohol can ruin your life. While customers browse, Pauline Egoak stares out the window of her brother's store and remembers the poster that was in the library when she was still in school a year ago. She imagines that it's still there.

It shows a boy and a girl, attractive teenagers, under the headline SWEET NOTHINGS. "If you love me, you will," whispers the boy, and the girl says, "Whoa!" "I promise you won't get pregnant." "Whoa!" replies the girl. "You're not gonna get AIDS," he says. "Whoa!"

"Just say WHOA to sex, too soon," the poster advises. "Three teenage girls in Alaska give birth every day. Know when to say WHOA before it's too late. Take your time. Don't buy that line."

Pauline is familiar with that line, because that's exactly what her boyfriend, Sam Michael, said to her over Christmas. And she bought his line, anyway, because what difference does it make? The church teaches abstinence, and Father Frank preaches that sex outside of marriage is a sin, but the young people ignore him. What does he know, a priest, a *kass'aq?* Her parents wouldn't say much, because she believes they'd be happy if she had a baby and gave it to them to raise. Several of her friends are either pregnant or have had babies. What else is there to do here, anyway?

Maybe Sam will marry her, but Pauline is not too optimistic about that. Last year when they were high school seniors he went on a career-planning trip. A counselor from Bethel escorted a group of kids from all over the school district to visit colleges and Job Corps sites in Alaska to consider career options. When he came back Sam was all fired up about going to college and studying to be a lawyer. And he actually did get into college, but when he came home for Christmas break he told her he didn't like it. He said he got homesick for the village, that everything outside is different and strange.

They got together after the trip to Shnamute, and she forgot all about saying "Whoa." She was thinking that Sam might meet some girl over there in Fairbanks and forget about her. And anyway, why does it always have to be the girl's job to say "Whoa"? So she did it. Now she hasn't heard from Sam since he went back.

Adeline lays a crumpled dollar bill and a candy bar on the counter and smiles up at her. Pauline hesitates and places a somewhat shriveled orange next to the candy. "For you," she says. "It's healthier."

CHAPTER 6

March

Amelia Joe, Adeline's great-grandmother, sits on the floor of the classroom, surrounded by yards and yards of inflated seal intestine. The school has declared this Yup'ik Culture Week, and Amelia has come to show the students how to make a seal-gut parka. Hardly anybody makes them anymore, except Amelia. Adeline's mother and grandmother say that it takes too much time, that it's easier to order a raincoat from the catalog and that *kass'aq* raincoats are better—you don't have to keep them damp all the time so they won't shrivel up.

But seal-gut parkas are warmer, Amelia tells the wide-eyed fifth- and sixth-graders, and lighter weight and more comfortable, and they keep you very dry. They last longer than plastic or rubber, if you take care of them. Best of all, they don't cost anything—the seal gives them to you! The only cost is your time, and Amelia has plenty of that.

Speaking softly in Yup'ik, Amelia explains that first she scraped and washed the intestine in urine. (No one is surprised at that; human urine has all kinds of uses—as medicine, of course, but also to ice sled runners and to quick-thaw a frozen mechanical part. And it's always available.) Then the cleaned intestines were blown up, tied off, and hung up to dry on Amelia's clothesline.

Now she cuts open the intestine tube to form a strip about four inches wide and demonstrates how she sews the strips together horizontally to make the body of the parka. She uses dental floss to stitch the seams together over a strand of wild grass that keeps the floss from pulling through the gut, explaining that *her* mother used animal sinew instead of floss. The grass expands when it gets wet and seals the many seams. Sewing together enough strips for a coat is a long, tedious process.

For this special visit to the school, Amelia is wearing a birdskin parka, made for her many years ago by her own mother. Hardly anybody knows how to make them anymore, either, she tells the children wistfully. "But," she says, glancing at her great-granddaughter Adeline, "if anybody here wants to make a seal-gut raincoat, I will be glad to help."

Adeline is proud of Amelia's work, but she herself is more interested in making baskets. Whenever she has a chance, she runs over to visit her friend Rose, whose

Rain parkas made from seal intestine are warm, light—and rare. Today few women have the patience or skill to make them.

mother, Josephine, is one of the best basket makers in the village. Josephine is teaching the girls the basics of her craft.

Last spring Josephine took the girls out to gather clumps of winter-stained, wrinkled grass—only wild rye grass is flexible enough for basketry—to form the center core of the coil. Then, soon after the first frost, they picked new grass, blade by blade, and dried and split it for the sewing grass. Most of the sewing grasses are nearly white, but some have been dyed rich colors. Josephine, who learned from her mother and her mother's mother, sometimes makes her dyes from onion skins, coffee grounds, stinkweed, crowberries, and blueberries, and sometimes gets colors from crepe paper, new sweatshirts, and Hershey bar wrappers.

Josephine knots together the ends of several strands of winter grass to form the core. She threads a single blade of sewing grass through a big-eyed needle and sucks on the blade a little to soften and shape it. She begins to wrap it around and around the bundle of winter grass, stitching it over and over, working in more strands to keep the core smooth as she bends the core into a coil. She adds row after row, changing from white grass to dyed grass to make the design.

Adeline and Rose have learned to make the flat coil that forms the bottom of the basket. Next Josephine shows them how to build up the sides, flaring them out and then gradually tapering toward the opening at the

Baskets sewn from grass gathered from the tundra have been valued by collectors for many years.

top. She demonstrates how to work in the design of red and green ducks that march in rows around the basket. Some other time she'll teach the girls how to make the lid, before the top of the basket is finished, to make sure it fits snugly. Josephine's baskets are as graceful as sculptured vases, but Adeline is finding that hers is already growing a bit lopsided. She's also running out of patience; she can't imagine doing this day after day.

Although many Yup'ik women are skilled in the craft, basketry is not native to Alaska. The techniques were introduced by *kass'aq* traders and teachers, who thought it would be a good way for Native Alaskans to earn money. In the old days, Josephine recalls, when her mother's mother made baskets in the 1920s and 1930s, women decorated their baskets with the delicate skin taken from the legs of birds and dyed dark colors.

Josephine works a few hours each day, taking ten days to two weeks to finish a basket. She packs it up and mails it to a man in Anchorage who says he will buy everything she makes. He sells them to tourists for high prices, but sometimes a visitor to the village who knows about Josephine's work buys one directly from her, and she gets more than twice what the dealer pays her.

Josephine says she is proudest of the basket purchased by the school and displayed in the glass case in the front hall, next to the basketball and Battle of the Books trophies. Rose confides to Adeline that her dream is someday to make a basket so beautiful that the school will buy hers, too.

Dennis has no interest in making baskets—that's for girls—but he loves to watch Paul Kasak carve ivory. For many years Paul has come down from a village to the north to demonstrate ivory carving to the students.

Ivory from the gigantic tusks of the walrus is scarce here. A few years ago there was a scandal when Native Alaskan poachers were caught on videotape, gunning down a herd of walrus on an ice floe and dumping the carcasses into the water. They sold the ivory tusks to souvenir manufacturers and were paid in drugs, which could be taken back to the villages and resold at huge profits. Villagers, shocked at the news, were outraged that the animals had been treated with such disrespect. Surely the *yua,* the soul, of the walrus was displeased. Ivory for carving comes from the occasional walrus killed by hunters for food.

Paul Kasak's specialty is lifelike carvings of animals of the tundra, a technique he learned from his father and his grandfather. In some villages carving disappeared completely when the Moravian missionaries forbade making images. Few men are left who remember how to work with ivory. Now Paul is an old man, and he hopes to pass on his skills to young people.

He spreads newspapers out on the schoolroom floor, and after he has shown them his tools and explained what each is for, he invites the students to try whittling bars of soap with a paring knife. Last year Dennis made a little boat; this year he works on a ptarmigan, a small bird. The soap is soft and easy to work with, and pretty soon he's got something that really does look like a ptarmigan. Dennis will take it home to his mother, to be put on the shelf with Adeline's partly finished basket and other things the children in the family have made.

Halfway through Yup'ik Culture Week, Martha Kiyutelluk, the village expert in skin sewing, comes to visit. In the past it was the work of every Eskimo woman to do all the skin sewing for her family. Each member of the family needed at least one fur parka, the fur on the inside for warmth, the carefully fitted hood edged with a ruff of wolverine. And of course they needed mukluks. "Mukluk" means "large seal" in Yup'ik and has become the *kass'aq* word for the sealskin boot. Yup'iks call boots by a variety of other names, depending on the style and function.

Martha brings two pairs of mukluks with her. She is working on one of them, a pair of plain, serviceable boots, made to stop just below the knee, with a cloth cuff and drawstring around the top to keep out the snow and cold air and thongs that cross over the foot and wrap around the ankle. She explains how she cuts the skins and pleats the toe of the hairless bottom sole with tiny crimps after dampening the skin to make it pliable—her own mother used to chew the skins to soften them. Then she demonstrates how she stitches the sole to the rough-haired uppers with dental floss.

The second pair is ready to be shipped to a customer in San Francisco. Martha has designed them with inlays of black and white calfskin purchased from a supplier and a beaded border around the top. Russian traders first brought beads, which the Yup'ik Eskimos used to make elaborate dangling earrings and labrets, worn through the lower lip, for both men and women. Some women pierced the septum, the center membrane of the nose, so they could wear nose beads. Labrets are out, but earrings, necklaces, and bracelets made of the tiny, bright-colored beads are popular, and beadwork is used to decorate dance fans and mukluks.

The students examine these special mukluks, admiring the skill with which they were made. "Imagine these mukluks," Adeline whispers in awe, "crossing the Golden Gate Bridge!"

All week the old men have been wandering in and out of the school gym, watching the progress on the kayak, offering advice, remembering. The gym has become like an old-time *qasgiq,* the men's house where kayaks were built and tools repaired. Most of the men now hunt and fish from aluminum boats with outboard motors, although there are still several wooden boats in use. Kayaks are mostly found in museums.

Mr. Kiyutelluk is in charge of the restoration project. His sons carried in the remains of his ancient boat, stripped off the old sealskin covering, and repaired the wooden frame, lashing each rib to a crosspiece. Six families contributed new sealskins, and under the direction of Mrs. Kiyutelluk the women sewed the damp skins together with sinew. The men pulled the skin covering over the frame, and now they're sewing it in place. When they're finished, they'll rub it inside and out with warm oil to keep the skins from shrinking.

Students come by to watch and to ask questions, and the elders are glad to tell them about the Old Days, when men hunted in kayaks. The hunter sat inside the opening, shaped like a barrel hoop. He wore a raincoat made of seal intestine—the kind Adeline's great-grandmother makes—tied tightly around the hoop and around his face, so that he formed one unit with the boat. He knew how to roll over in the kayak, tipping over to one side and coming up on the other, so that if the water got rough he would not drown.

The kayak is good, the elder tells the students. These lightweight skin boats are easy to maneuver, and they can go many places that wooden and aluminum boats can't. You can carry them, if you have to, and there's no outboard motor to quit on you. There's plenty of space inside, room for several small seals, and once you've tied up your raincoat again, if you happen to tip over, you won't lose the seals.

Down the hall from the gymnasium where the men talk about hunting, rock music blares from a radio above the whir of sewing machines as a group of high school girls rush to finish their *qaspeqs* in time for the Friday night program.

An overblouse made of bright cotton, the *qaspeq* was originally worn as a parka cover. It has one wide pocket in the front and a deep ruffle around the bottom. Little girls wear them until they get old enough to prefer sweatshirts and T-shirts. Old women wear them because they are traditional. Some younger women like them because they're practical. Now a group of high school girls has

Little girls and traditional older women still wear *qaspeqs* of bright-colored cotton.

decided to make matching *qaspeqs* for their dance team, which will make its debut Friday night.

It was Marcia Prescott's idea to form a team, instructed once a week by Agnes's grandmother and her great-aunt, and Marcia's idea to make matching *qaspeqs* for the dancers. Lucy volunteered to help, and she's brought her own sewing machine to the school. Adeline has been given the job of pinning white rickrack on Alice Bean's blue *qaspeq.* Adeline isn't old enough to be on the team, although she's been going to the community center every week to dance with her grandmother since she was in kindergarten. Last year her grandmother gave her a beautiful headdress decorated with beads and feathers. Next year, Adeline tells herself, sticking herself with a pin, she'll be dancing with them, too.

Only Yup'ik will be spoken on the final night of Cultural Week. That will leave out the *kass'aq* teachers and even a few people, like Alice, who moved to Chaputnguak from villages near Bethel where Yup'ik has almost disappeared. Walter, the principal, has agreed; he's proud of his school's bilingual program.

There are two modern Eskimo-language families, Yup'ik and Inuit, as different from each other as German and English, and because the Eskimo population is small and widely scattered, there are many dialects.

Eskimo is a polysynthetic language, meaning that an enormous number of modifiers can be added, like building blocks, at the end or in the middle (but rarely at the beginning) of a basic word to give it a complete meaning. The result is one very long word that can convey the same meaning as a whole sentence in English. A simple noun may have thirty-six endings; a verb can take more than six hundred forms. Eskimo is far more precise than English or most other European languages: one word, for instance, can describe the exact quality of snow on the tundra at a given moment or the exact location of a seal on the ice. Here is a Yup'ik word from a textbook: *qusngirngalngurpagtangqerrsugnarquq.* It means, "There seems to be a big goat."

Before the arrival of white people in the Arctic, there was no written Eskimo language. Missionaries introduced the Roman alphabet in the eighteenth century, and from this a written language was eventually derived. Language experts have tried to develop consistency in the written language. Many words once commonly spelled with a *k* are now written with a *q,* which more closely represents the sound. *Kayak,* for example, now a common English word, is no longer spelled that way in Yup'ik; instead, it is spelled *qayaq.*

The Yup'ik alphabet is similar to English, but it contains only eighteen letters; *b, d, f, h, j, o, x,* and *z* are missing. Some vowels can be written double for a "long sound": *aa, ii, uu.* And sometimes the consonant is doubled in pronunciation but not in spelling; instead, an apostrophe is added, as in the word *Yup'ik.*

Yup'ik is a difficult language for most English-speaking people to master, not because of the complex grammar but because the sounds are so different from English sounds. Like German, many Yup'ik sounds are produced in the throat. The letter *q* appears often in Yup'ik, similar to the *k* sound in English but made further back in the throat. The *r* is like a French *r* and sounds nothing like an English *r.* Some people describe the language as sounding "juicy."

In spite of the difficulties, a *kass'aq* (pronounced,

roughly, GUSS-uk) usually manages to pick up a few words. *Camai,* for example, pronounced cha-MY, means "welcome" or "greetings." *Quyana,* pronounced koo-YAH-nah, means "thank you." *Yup'ik,* of course, is YOOP-ik.

When Adeline's parents were children, the federal government ran the schools and had an "English only" policy. Jim remembers when he was not allowed to speak Yup'ik in school; the teachers slapped his hands with a ruler if he did. When he was in third grade a more enlightened teaching couple arrived. They did not punish Yup'ik but they rewarded English. Children who remembered to speak only English around their teachers collected a quarter at the end of the week. Jim tried hard to learn English, and he was ashamed that his parents spoke it so poorly.

In villages near white population centers like Bethel, the teachers were quite successful—the Yup'ik language has all but disappeared in those places. But in remote and isolated villages like Chaputnguak, Yup'ik is still the first language children learn. The village elders want to keep it that way. The old people speak Yup'ik almost exclusively; their heavily accented English is for *kass'aq* teachers, doctors, and Father Frank.

Adeline and her brothers and sisters spoke only Yup'ik when they started going to school. But gradually they learned English, too, and now they get instruction in both languages so that they'll know how to read and write English as well as Yup'ik. Leon, the Yup'ik teacher, comes to Adeline's classroom once a day. Just before Culture Week began, he printed a few words on the chalkboard: *kalukaq uqiquq nakaciuq.*

"What does the first word mean?" Leon asked in English, and Adeline answered, "It's like a big party—a feast." And the second word? "Seal party." But she was less certain about the third.

"*Nakaciuq* was the number-one festival in the village long ago," Leon explained, switching to Yup'ik.

Back and forth the class flew between the two languages, the two cultures, the two worlds. But this Friday night for a little while, perhaps, there will be only one.

PART 2
Breakup

The sun is moving north. Every day it emerges a few minutes earlier, at a point a few degrees farther north on the horizon, and there are twelve hours of daylight.

The temperature rises more quickly inland than it does near the coast, and the thaw works its way toward the ocean. Dark patches of shrubs and lichens are beginning to erupt through the snow. Snow machine trails are wet and bare. Soon now—it can happen any time from the end of March to late May or even early June—the river ice will groan and shriek as it breaks apart and starts its annual move down to the sea. At Bethel breakup occurs about May 14, on the average. All over Alaska people bet money on the exact minute when the ice of the big rivers will begin to move.

Breakup is a momentous happening in the Far North,

one of the turning points of the year, signaling the end of winter. The tundra changes from an unbroken expanse of frozen wasteland, where exposure can mean painful frostbite in seconds and death in minutes, to a spongy marsh where wildlife breeds in profusion and grasses and flowering plants show off their splendid colors during the brief, intense growing season. At the other side of the year, freeze-up—the second crucial but more subtle turning point—transforms the tundra to featureless whiteness again.

In winter snowmobiles race over the frozen ponds and rivers as easily as they do over the frozen tundra, but breakup, when it comes, changes that. For a few weeks transportation will be a problem, as the tundra shifts from winter to that second season of the arctic year, the quick succession of spring, summer, and fall. Then it will be a world of outboard motorboats on the rivers, four-wheelers on the boardwalk, and muddy walking on the tundra, of taking the long way around the pond.

Life in the villages changes with the turn in the seasons. For weeks the men of Chaputnguak and other villages near the Bering Sea have been taking their snow machines out over the shelf ice to open water to hunt seals. But soon the shelf ice will begin to break off and move out to sea, the men will put their boats into the water between the ice floes, and the hunting will begin in earnest, day after long day. It is a dangerous business, but their food supply depends on it, as it has for thousands

Ice on the river after breakup each spring floods the villages and makes travel more difficult but heralds the coming of milder weather.

of years. By this time of year most of the caches of native food have been used up, and everyone is tired of *kass'aq* food. They yearn for the taste of fresh seal meat.

David wakes during the night and listens to the eerie sounds from the river. For several days the ice has cracked and heaved; now, finally, it has begun to move. Spring truly begins the day the ice goes out.

CHAPTER 7
April

Gray morning, overcast sky, barely daylight. Two dozen boats loaded with guns, CB radios, gas, tools, harpoons, tarps, food, binoculars, and extra motors rest on the icebound beach. The hunters ease the boats into the black water, climb aboard—two or three in each boat—and start the kickers, the outboard motors. Judson's uncles, Pete and Andy, have agreed to take him, even though it's a school day, which is why Jim isn't going. The school cook can't be truant.

Yesterday the men studied the sky and read in it the signs they had been waiting for: a reflection of the sea that told them the shelf ice had broken off and the leads (pronounced LEEDS), the channels between the ice floes, were open. In a few more weeks most of the ice will have moved out to sea, but now there are still huge floes that

Seal hunting is no less dangerous—or rewarding—today with a powerful motorboat than it was years ago with a kayak.

can suddenly drift together and crush one of the boats like an egg. Still, hunting is less dangerous now than just before breakup, when the men still drove their snow machines far out on the ice, risking the chance that a piece might break off and carry away one of the expensive machines or one of the hunters. Sometimes the ice drifts back and the machine or the hunter can be rescued; sometimes it doesn't. There have been no hunting fatalities in Chaputnguak for years, although several snow machines lie at the bottom of the Bering Sea, but last year in a village to the north a young man was marooned on the ice for a week. He survived, but both his feet had to be amputated and the ordeal affected his mind.

Sitting in the eighteen-foot aluminum boat driven by a fifty-horsepower kicker, Judson nervously fingers his powerful .222 rifle, his Christmas gift. This is the first time he has been allowed to go seal hunting this early in the spring. When he was younger, he had gone out with his uncles only after the ice had cleared and most of the danger was past. The sense of danger and the hope that today he will get his first big seal are exhilarating. But he sits motionless and silent while Pete maneuvers the boat among the drifting ice floes.

The seals, like the hunters, have been waiting for breakup. All winter they stayed under the ice, feeding on the few fish available, coming up regularly to their breathing holes. Soon now they will wriggle up on land to bear their pups and to breed again, but now they swim freely in the leads, their streamlined heads breaking the surface of the dark water, disappearing instantly at the slightest sound.

Pete cuts the motor; the men paddle silently among the floes. In the far distance they hear the faint crack of a rifle shot. No one speaks. They study the water and push away floating pieces of ice that might clunk against the boat. Judson's gaze wanders and then halts suddenly. He motions to Pete. Pete nods and waits for the seal to come closer. If he shoots at this distance the seal, thin from a long winter of poor eating, may sink before they can get to it.

Although he itches to try, Judson knows that he must not fire. That right belongs to only one man at a time in each boat—otherwise it would be dangerous—and it was agreed this morning that Pete would be first. The seal disappears suddenly; when it comes up again it is farther away, not closer. Pete curses softly and lowers his rifle.

The morning passes. They hear more shots from the other boats, and they spot several more seals. Only one is close enough to shoot but not close enough to reach, and by the time they get there it has sunk from sight, leaving a bloom of blood in the water.

At noon they stop to eat and rest, dropping anchor and lighting the little Primus stove in the boat to make tea. They share their lunch of pilot bread and smoked salmon dipped in seal oil and sprinkled with salt. Judson eats and eats. The men tease him about his huge appetite as they pack away what's left.

Although there was not much wind when the hunters started at dawn, it is blowing hard now and the water is choppy. Andy tells Judson that he can make the next shot, and Judson feels a line of sweat break out on his upper lip. An hour passes, two hours. He knows the seals are all around him and that he must wait.

A sleek head breaks the surface of the water only a few yards away. His uncle nods. Judson tries to sight carefully, his breath sucked in, but the heaving boat keeps spoiling his aim. What he wants is a head shot, but the seal is swimming away, and Judson knows that he must make his shot *now.* He braces himself and squeezes the trigger. The sound of the shot startles him, and so does the jerk of the animal's head. He got it!

As quickly as they can—the water is rougher and the leads are narrow now—they rush to the seal and plunge a harpoon into it. It is a large one, and Judson has shot it cleanly in the shoulder. Nobody says much, even after they haul it into the boat and see the size of it. It would not be like them to show excitement, but Judson can tell they are proud of him. Not long after, Pete gets a seal, too, and they decide to turn back before the weather gets worse.

The return trip is slow. The sea lifts their boat to the crest of each wave and then dashes it into a trough of water, time after time. Spray drenches them, and the harsh wind drives the damp cold into their bones. At last they drag their boat up on the beach, load the seals on the sled, and start home.

The whole village knows that it was a good day and that Judson has gotten his first seal. The hunters had sent word to the village by radio, and since nearly every home has a telephone or a CB or both, the word spread quickly. Lucy, delighted with the news of Judson's success, has begun to plan the celebration. David chews on a mixture of excitement and envy.

David is not allowed to go hunting—not yet. Later in the spring after the ice has cleared his father and uncles may invite him. Only when they are sure he can take care of himself and be a real help will he be allowed to go out for early spring seal hunting.

But David, at thirteen, is already a good shot. Like the other boys his age, he has been shooting at things for more than half his life. When he was small he learned to use a slingshot, and by the time he was six he could pick off an occasional target with an air rifle. At eight he got his first bird, a ptarmigan, and his family celebrated with a big party. Since then he has been helping to supply his mother with birds for the soup pot.

As soon as school was out today, David rushed home and picked up his .22 rifle, slung a sack over his shoulder, and started out to meet his friend Mike to go duck hunting. In April the sky is full of migrating waterfowl, and David brought down four ducks without much trouble—the only trouble being that shooting ducks from March through September is illegal, according to the Migratory Bird Treaty Act of 1918, a law that if it were enforced would interfere with the Yup'iks' food gathering. Fortunately, the courts have decided that it's all right for Yup'iks to shoot migrating ducks for food (but not threatened kinds of geese). But there is still a lot of confusion about what is legal and what is not.

Before he and Mike went home, they stopped to visit Amelia, David's great-grandmother, and each gave her one of his ducks. David and the other boys always take her something when they come back from hunting or gathering eggs. This is not just a kind gesture to an elderly relative; taking food to old women is an ancient custom that supposedly brings luck to young hunters. And Amelia has promised David that when he gets his first seal, she will make him one of her famous seal-gut parkas. She thanked the boys for the ducks, and they took the rest home to their mothers. Lucy greeted David with the news of Judson's seal.

Lucy cleaned the ducks, feeding the entrails to Bingo, the dog, and carefully plucking out the feathers, but everything else, including the feet and head, went into the pot with water and onions and a handful of rice. She set the pot on the stove to simmer and her cooking was done for the day. When Judson gets home, she will butcher his seal. Preparing food for storage is a big job for the village women, but cooking it is not. Some food is eaten raw; the rest is boiled with a minimum of fuss.

Now Lucy feeds the last of the family wash through the electric wringer and begins to plan a seal party, *uqiquq,* to celebrate Judson's prize. According to the radio report, one of the other families got the biggest seal of the hunt—the first big seal of the season requires a special celebration—but Lucy will put on a party for the women of the village because this is Judson's first large seal. She must spend at least a couple of hundred dollars, more than she can afford, to avoid gossip and a reputation of stinginess, especially since her family is among the wealthiest in the village: her husband has a full-time job and a steady income, and her uncle owns the village store. Besides, seal parties are part of the social tradition of the village. Having a party when a seal is killed is a way of sharing, and sharing is basic to Yup'ik life.

But there is no more time now to think about it. Dennis has just rushed in and announced breathlessly that he and his friends have been watching over by the airstrip, and he's seen the headlights in the distance. The hunters are on their way in.

Jim comes out to help Judson drag home his seal. David and Dennis are there, too, full of curiosity. Judson tries not to show how tired he is, but when Lucy tells him there is a pot of duck soup on the stove, he gladly follows Jim to the table. Jim and Judson set the pot between them, dipping in with their hands for chunks of meat and spooning up the rich broth.

Lucy has sharpened her *uluaq,* the "woman's knife" with its broad rounded blade and a wooden handle at the top. She has called her mother-in-law, Liz, on the CB to help with the butchering. The carcass lies on a piece of cardboard in the middle of the kitchen floor. Judson placed his shot well, so the whole skin can be used. Lucy slits the seal down the middle from the chin and flenses off the skin and *muqtuq*—blubber, the underlying layer of fat—in one piece. Then she separates the *muqtuq* from the skin, a more complicated job, and slices the fat into large strips. Finally she cuts the meat up into big chunks, all to be given out tomorrow at the seal party. Liz cleans the intestines, pouring water through them, a job traditionally taken over by the old women. The intestines will be boiled and eaten, and the flippers will be made into soup. Nothing is wasted.

Even after the meat is distributed at a seal party, there will still be plenty to do. Pete also got a seal, and Liz will turn the whole skin inside out and make a poke, a bag for storing fish or fat that has been rendered and melted down to oil. Seal oil, fresh or fermented, is eaten with practically everything. In a few weeks the women in the

The sealskin poke, a whole skin turned inside out, is still used for storing fish and seal oil.

village will start cutting up the meat from the seals that the men bring in nearly every day and prepare for drying the thousands of pounds of meat that are accumulating on porches and in storage sheds. Lucy and Liz work as a team on the long, tedious job, processing about a hundred pounds of meat and oil in a day. Some of it is eaten fresh, the rest dried on racks to eat during the late summer and fall.

Adeline helps, mostly running errands for her mother and grandmother. She also watches, and sometimes her mother will let her try the beginner's job of cutting the fat and skin from the flesh. Although she knows that when she grows up it will be part of her job to butcher the seals her husband kills, Adeline hopes that she will be lucky and marry someone who has a regular job, like her father. Then there won't be so many seals and so much work.

Up since 4:00 A.M., Judson is asleep that night before his head hits the pillow. At four o'clock the next morning he crawls out of his sleeping bag and starts to dress. It's Saturday, and Jim is going hunting, too. He hands Judson a plate of fried eggs and pours them both some coffee. While they sip the hot coffee, they zip insulated pants over jeans and long underwear and pull on heavy boots. Between bites of pilot bread spread with margarine, they collect their rifles and ammunition. Then they put on parkas and gloves and go out to meet Pete and Andy.

During this season while the seals are migrating north, the men will hunt nearly every day, from daybreak until late at night. It may be after midnight before they've had supper and a steam and fall into bed. A few hours later they will be up again. If there are a lot of seals, the younger boys are taken out and taught to hunt. David, of course, is hoping for a bountiful season.

Lucy gets up early, too, to get ready for the seal party. She has decided to bake bread in the bread machine she bought Jim for Christmas, and she will also serve her guests *akutaq,* Crisco whipped with berries.

Lucy hurries over to the store, but today she's a customer, not a clerk. She's not the only customer; there will be other seal parties today, and the store is crowded. She collects the gifts she'll distribute to her guests: canned fruit, crackers, cookies, boxes of cake mix, candy, dried soup, tea bags, apples and oranges and even some bananas flown out from Bethel in anticipation of the parties. Next the useful little items: shoelaces, candles, flashlight batteries, thimbles, matches, sponges. She picks up cans of coffee and sacks of flour, rice, and sugar.

Then she buys a length of cotton and corduroy fabric, a mop head, a set of kitchen spoons, a package of underpants, a box of tampons, cards of rickrack trimming, plus some big boxes of soap powder and a few cans of snuff. She does not have cash to pay for all of it; her cousin will add it to her account and deduct it from her wages.

The guests—who are not related to Judson, because

this is to show that he is a good hunter and able to provide someday for a wife—are invited by telephone and CB radio, and late in the morning they begin to gather outside Lucy's house, perhaps forty women and a dozen or so little children. By tradition no men are present—not even the hunter being honored. Inside to help her are Lucy's own relatives: her mother, sister—the sister from Bethel, Judson's birth mother, was invited to the celebration but couldn't come out in time—a half dozen aunts, cousins, and nieces, and Adeline, who has skipped school to help out. Lucy and her mother carry the tubs of blubber and seal meat outside, and the party is on. The guests come forward a few at a time, with smiles and greetings, and each gets a share of the meat in her bucket and a slice of homemade bread and a portion of *akutaq* in her bowl.

When the meat and blubber have been distributed, Lucy brings out a special bundle, a pillowcase holding a mink pelt, a pair of brightly checked polyester slacks, and a few other choice items. The women crowd together, and Lucy throws the bundle up over their heads, hoping that it will be caught by one person and not argued over by several. The bundle drops into the hands of one of the younger women. She is well liked, and everyone seems satisfied that she is the one to get it.

When Lucy and her mother are ready to give out the bulk items—sugar, flour, coffee, rice, and soap powder—the women surge forward again, this time carrying little bags or squares of plastic. Some of the older women who are wearing *qaspeqs* collect each handful in a separate part of the deep ruffle around the bottom of the parka cover and tie it up with pieces of string.

Then comes the free-for-all. Standing on the steps Lucy begins to toss small items out over the heads of the crowd, ending with pieces of cloth, bundles of string, and lengths of yarn. The women jump, push, squeal, and grab, except for the old ladies who sit placidly out of the way waiting for Lucy or her sister to hand them something. And then the party, which has lasted less than an hour, is over. But there will be more seals—hundreds of them—more work, more parties.

The Yup'ik word for man is *angun,* literally "a device for chasing and catching food." Thirty or forty years ago in Chaputnguak and the other Yup'ik villages people lived almost entirely on what they could shoot, catch, or gather, and they sold or bartered furs and ivory carvings and baskets for the few other things they needed. The subsistence lifestyle—hunting, fishing, and foraging—is still the way most people live in the coastal villages. But today there is a difference: cash.

Yup'iks have learned that subsistence living is expensive—each family spends an average of three thousand dollars a year for hunting and fishing equipment. Only the wealthy men in the village can afford the snow machines, aluminum boats, outboard motors, gasoline, guns, ammunition; poorer families can't afford the subsistence lifestyle, and they must rely on food that is cheaper to catch, like tomcod and smelt, and often end up with food stamps and welfare. These days it is not enough to be *angun,* a device to chase and catch. As Judson is becoming more and more aware, you need a job, too.

CHAPTER 8

May

The girls walk slowly, eyes on the ground, searching for the nests of wild birds. Tommy tags along behind, scrambling over patches of snow and mounds of crowberry, Labrador tea, and reindeer moss. Agnes, Adeline, and Katie are putting eggs in their buckets lined with moss, but Tommy doesn't find a thing.

Suddenly he jumps back, startled. He has nearly stepped on a ptarmigan, a kind of grouse with plumage that makes it very hard to spot: in winter its feathers are completely white, but by the middle of May they have turned a mottled brown that blends perfectly with the ground. Although they are land birds and not good fliers, most migrate further north to lay their eggs. But this one has nested a hundred yards from his home, and Tommy has found it. The ptarmigan takes off in a whir of wings, and Tommy shouts for his sisters. Agnes and Katie hug and kiss him, and Adeline helps him put the eggs, still in the nest, in his bucket. All the eggs are fertile—later in the season the embryo chicks will be well developed in other eggs they find—but Lucy will boil them and they'll eat them, embryos and all.

Katie is already an accomplished egg hunter, having found her first nest when she was barely four. There had been a party, *uqiquq,* to celebrate; the proven ability to provide food is reason for celebration in every Yup'ik village. Sometimes a small child gets a little help in finding eggs for the first time; Tommy didn't need any. Now he will have his *uqiquq.*

That ends the egg hunting for today; they're anxious to hurry home to report Tommy's success. Another day Adeline will pack a lunch and go egg hunting with her friends. They will fan out over the tundra, combing the area thoroughly. Next month when the weather is warmer, the whole family—except for the baby Lilly, but including their grandmother Liz—will go by boat to a good nesting area out along the coast. Gathering eggs of certain migrating waterfowl is technically against the law, but like shooting ducks, it's allowed since it is for food.

It's a perfect day for storyknifing—not too wet, not too dry—and so after school Agnes and Katie and their friend Tina squat down on the riverbank and spend the next couple of hours telling knife stories.

Agnes smooths a space in the mud and begins to draw with her knife, which she carries with her in her jacket pocket. First she sketches the outline of a house furnished with rectangles and circles to represent a stove, table, chairs, beds, and washbasin, just like her own home. Then she draws characters in the house—symbols for Mother, Father, Grandmother, Girl—and describes what is happening in the scene. As she finishes each scene, she erases the sketch from the mud with her knife and sets up a new scene. Katie listens intently to her sister's tale of a grandmother who goes out to gather eggs, which is one of Katie's favorite things to do.

Tina takes her turn. Her story is about a little boy who has been playing "string story," even though his parents have told him to stop playing and go to sleep. Tommy, who is watching, smiles—he likes to play string story, too. Little brothers are not allowed to participate in storyknifing, although it's okay to watch.

Years ago fathers carved a *yaaruin,* story knife, out of driftwood or walrus tusk for their daughters. Tina's father cut and filed a strip of metal banding used to secure building materials to make her knife; Agnes uses her mother's stainless steel butter knife. Little girls begin telling knife tales when they are about five, and the stories get more complicated as the girls get older. Adeline, who at eleven is almost too old for storyknifing, likes to tell really scary stories, or ones about her dreams.

The knife tale is found only in the Yukon-

Kuskokwim Delta, where Yup'ik is spoken. Some of the tales are traditional, but often the girls make up stories. In old-time Yup'ik society knife tales were about hunting, fishing, and food gathering. Today, in those villages where storyknifing has not disappeared, many of the stories have to do with shopping at the village store. But what used to be a daily activity for young girls has been replaced by TV and videos in most villages—including Chaputnguak.

Boys might tell string stories, knotting a piece of string into a loop and manipulating it on their fingers to form all sorts of complicated figures, similar to the cat's cradle. But no boy would ever tell a knife story or handle a story knife.

There is a superstition that a boy who uses a girl's things will be unlucky in hunting. Men don't use women's belongings or do women's work, and they won't allow women to leave their traditional role. Pauline Egoak has been trying for months to talk one of her brothers into taking her hunting, but none of them will do it, afraid he'll be teased by the others. Nevertheless, she has taught herself to be a pretty good shot, borrowing Larry's rifle and going out to the dump to shoot at cans and the birds that hang around the garbage. But Pauline knows she'll never be allowed to go seal hunting; that would be too much to ask.

Men are considered naturally superior to women, and

Girls developed a sense of balance by jostling each other off a seesaw. Some activities, like storyknifing, have virtually disappeared.

although women have gained more influence, few have any official voice. Because of the rigors of arctic life, survival once depended on clearly defined roles. Man was the hunter, and hunting required a strength and endurance that women are thought not to have. Then someone had to prepare the food and clothing from the hunter's catch. It was the man's work to bring home the seal; as soon as it was brought into the porch of the house, it became the property of the woman who skinned and butchered it. She prepared the meat for cooking, the intestines for sewing into a raincoat or the window of a sod house, the blubber for eating and for the oil lamp that provided light and heat. And, of course, she bore and took care of the children. Without a husband, a woman had no food. Without a wife, a man had no clothing.

In the old days a hunter considered his wife of little importance as a person. If a woman tried to harpoon an animal herself, the hunters believed that other animals would stay away and that everyone would starve. In subsistence hunting, luck is as important as skill, and no one could afford to risk bad luck. Today, there are other ways besides hunting to put food on the table: cash from jobs, food stamps from the government when cash is short, welfare when there is no cash at all. But the old attitudes of male superiority do not die. This can create bad feelings when it's the wife who has the steady-paying job and brings in most of the family's cash.

When Lucy was in high school, few Yup'ik girls were encouraged to have careers. It was assumed that a girl would help out at home until she married, and then she would help her husband. Lucy never felt bad about dropping out of boarding school. Boys, on the other hand, were urged to finish school and get good jobs. But things have changed; Lucy is determined that her daughters as well as her sons will finish high school—at least now they can do that without leaving the village—and then go to college. For now she tries not to think about what getting an education means: they'll have to leave the village, and maybe the delta, to find a job.

Pauline's cousin Olivia is getting married. The bride's father invited everyone to the church one Saturday afternoon for the wedding. Olivia and her parents and her eighteen-month-old daughter, Melissa, and other relatives enter the church and sit near the front. Olivia wears new pants and the beautiful jeweled sweater that Michael has giver her. Michael, handsome in his National Guard uniform, comes in later with his friends and sits in back with them. When Father Frank arrives, the bridal couple and their witnesses—Pauline, who holds Melissa in her arms, and Michael's brother Steve—gather in front of the altar, and the Roman Catholic ceremony begins in English and Yup'ik. In the middle of her parents' vows, Melissa starts to chatter. Someone takes snapshots during the ceremony.

Afterward Olivia's family gives a dinner at the community center. A towering cake with a miniature bride and groom on the top has been flown out from Bethel, but it was a rough landing, and the cake got bashed in on one side. Olivia and Michael cut it with a kitchen knife tied with a big white bow, the way Olivia saw it in a bride's magazine, and serve pieces to the guests to eat with their *akutaq.* There are more snapshots, to put in the album Pauline bought them as a wedding gift.

Then Michael and Olivia and Melissa go home to Olivia's parents' house, where Michael has been living for the past year, to begin official married life and to hope that someday they'll have a home of their own.

Before missionaries came to the villages, marriage was a simple thing. When a young Yup'ik was a proven hunter and ready to take on the responsibilities of a wife and family, his parents picked out a young girl to be his wife, talked it over with her parents, and if everyone agreed, the young man moved in with the girl. They lived there until they had children and established a home of their own. If it didn't work out—if the wife was not a good butcher and skin sewer, or if she didn't have children—the husband left.

When the priests came, all that changed. The church does not approve of arranged marriages, and Father Frank makes sure the couple have known each other for several months before he lets them get married. Before the wedding one of the older women of the village, in this case Lucy Koonuk, invited Olivia for a visit. While the two sipped tea, Lucy lectured Olivia on the responsibilities of marriage: she must understand her role as a helper to her husband and a mother to the child they already have as well as the ones sure to come. This form of premarital counseling is traditional in the village. One of the older men took Michael aside and talked to him about the importance of the step he was about to take, reminding him of his duties to his wife and children.

Early missionaries had a lot of convincing to do when they first reached the Yup'iks, whom they regarded as pagans entirely without morals. The bond between husband and wife was strong, but in the old days, wife lending was a common practice, a courtesy extended to friends and visitors just as one offered food and lodging. It was the husband's decision; a wife had no right to refuse to be part of her husband's hospitality or to offer it without his consent. The missionaries got used to many Eskimo customs, but not that one. Gradually the Christianized Yup'iks accepted *kass'aq* sexual standards. There is no more custom of wife lending, but sex still happens outside of marriage. The single mother could not have survived in old Yup'ik society, but she's not unusual today.

Yup'ik babies are constantly being held, walked, rocked, cuddled, talked to, bathed, and fed; they are hardly ever allowed to cry. They sleep with their parents from the time they are born, not only because of lack of space, but because the parents want to be sure they will know if the baby needs anything during the night. Even if Olivia had had a separate room for Melissa's crib, she would have been criticized by her relatives until she gave in and took the baby back into her own bed.

Jim and Lucy's youngest child, Lilly, at the age of two

and a half has total security. Her mother and sisters watch her carefully, in the house as well as outside on the board-walk, so that she can't hurt herself. As she begins to range farther, everyone will keep an eye on her. If Lilly gets into trouble as she grows up, she will seldom be spanked or even scolded harshly. Yup'ik children are not controlled by rules or disciplined by punishment but by patient lessons on "how to be good." If children want something, adults try to give it to them, believing that a child can't be "spoiled" too much. Yup'ik parents have a good reason for not hitting their children. To hit a child would be like hitting the dead relative for whom the child is named.

Dennis was given the name of Qetunraq for his father's uncle who died just before Dennis was born. When Dennis ruined his father's good hunting knife, he wasn't punished. Jim remembers too fondly the uncle who took him on his fishing boat when he was a boy to become angry at his uncle's spirit in his own son. Instead of yelling at Dennis, he simply pointed out the damage. It seems to work, for Yup'ik children are generally well behaved, soft-spoken, and respectful to their parents and elders.

When Jim and Lucy adopted Lucy's nephew Judson, they were following an old Yup'ik custom. Even in a society where babies are much wanted and loved and children are considered the most precious of life's riches, nearly every family in the village has at one time or another given away a child—when there was not enough money, or when there were just too many small children to be cared for properly, or for some other reason. And nearly every family has at some time adopted a child—usually a grandchild, niece, or nephew. The tie between the adoptive parents and the adopted child is as strong as the tie between biological parents and child. Some say the adopted child often becomes the special one in the family, the most favored. Jim and Lucy already had David, and Adeline was on the way, when five-year-old Judson needed parents. He doesn't feel that he's special, but he does know that he's loved.

"Pomp and Circumstance" booms out of the loud-speakers set up in the gym, and the video camera begins to record one of the most important events of the year: graduation. The name of each graduate has been made into a poster, ringed with snapshots and decorated with sparkly lettering. Seven preschoolers, including Tommy, dressed in miniature white caps and gowns, are coaxed to march beneath a decorated arch. They're followed by the eighth-graders, led by David, in blue gowns with white trim and white tassels on their mortarboards, who in turn are followed by the four graduating seniors with the school colors reversed, white gowns with blue trim. The last one in the lineup is Judson, the valedictorian.

His girlfriend, Alice, a junior, sits with Jim and Lucy, biting her lip. She knows that Judson will be leaving soon—next month—to work in a salmon cannery in

Bristol Bay, and at the end of the summer for college. He's been admitted to a technical school in Seattle, and it will be months before she sees him again. But Alice has plans, too: next year she will leave for Mt. Edgecumbe in Sitka and finish high school there. Then maybe she'll go to college, too. Alice wonders how strong the pull will be to return to the village. It depends partly on Judson.

Walter Prescott, dressed in an unfamiliar white shirt and coat and tie, says, "*Camai,* welcome," and continues in English. Then he turns the ceremony over to Wally Koonuk, the deacon, who delivers the invocation in Yup'ik. Next the president of the village council has quite a few words to say in Yup'ik. Finally the sound system offers a trumpet fanfare, and the graduates step forward one by one. Marcia Prescott, in a flowered dress, stockings, and heels, flashes each one a big smile. Walter shakes hands and presents the diploma. The graduate moves the tassel from one side of the mortarboard to the other, grins toward his or her family—somebody always snaps a picture—and then the wonderful, hoped-for moment is over.

Afterward, of course, there's a big party, but as she poses for pictures with Judson, Alice is already dreaming about next week and the prom.

The prom is just about all the high school kids have talked about for weeks. The whole school is invited, in fact the whole village is invited to the dance in the gym. The theme this year is to be Mexican Night. Jerry

Waterman has worked with the boys to cut out and paint giant cactuses and sombreros; the girls have been producing dozens of paper flowers. Tapes of mariachi music were ordered, and Marcia and Walter, who often vacation in Mexico, have agreed to loan the students a couple of brightly striped serapes for the crowning of the king and queen. And Jim Koonuk has promised them a Mexican meal as authentic as he can make it: tacos and enchiladas, chips and salsa, and something called guacamole.

Alice's blue lace prom dress and silver sandals have already arrived in the mail. Lucy managed to set aside money to buy Judson a suit and a white shirt, and at Alice's pleading she sent for a baby blue necktie that will exactly match the color of the blue lace dress. This is the night that Alice both dreams of and dreads, because when it's over it will be Alice's most cherished memory, and the memory will have to last a long time.

CHAPTER 9

June

Tender new growth covers the tundra, and the women and the girls and young children have begun their foraging trips. What was once a dead white landscape is now alive with low-growing vegetation, much of it important to the villagers' diet. All through the summer they will gather the green plants: willow leaves, wild celery, sour dock, wild rhubarb, ferns, wild spinach. Great-grandmother Amelia is looking especially for a kind of grass that she will braid and use to string up fish for drying.

As they walk, Amelia talks to Agnes about the different kinds of wildlife they see. Amelia knows the name of every bird in the sky, as well as its habits, but she is less sure about the plants. She simply knows which are good to eat and which are not. In the fall she'll be back again, looking for "mouse" holes. The "mice"—tundra lemmings—are also busy foraging and hoarding, and the old women are especially good at spotting their cache of tiny roots and underground stems that make such good soup.

Back home again with their baskets filled, the old woman and the young girl sit on the steps to rest and to eat a little of the wild celery, dipped in seal oil and sprinkled with salt. Some of the greens will be eaten fresh, and some will be lightly boiled and then preserved in seal oil for winter food. Just then Dennis swaggers in. "We're going muskrat hunting," he announces. "Grandfather is taking me tomorrow."

The next morning Dennis helps to pack overnight provisions into Charlie Koonuk's boat: tarps for making a tent, a stove for brewing tea, a supply of food, and the guns and ammunition. This is a chance to get some skins to sell, and—just as important—a lesson in shooting and gun safety for Dennis. They start up the river to one of the lakes where Grandfather says there will be plenty of muskrats. It's a long trip, but after they have found a high and fairly dry place to set up the camp and have fixed tea and had a bite to eat, they start the tiring walk over the marshy tundra to the lake. Charlie has brought his own gun and a .22 rifle for Dennis to use. Dennis guesses that if he does exactly as he is told and handles the rifle well, his grandfather might let him keep it.

The muskrats begin to come out of their holes late in the afternoon, and Dennis sees them swimming out on the lake, rippling the still surface of the water. His grandfather makes a sign; go ahead and try. Dennis picks one closest to him, squints along the rifle barrel, and squeezes off a shot. The bullet skips into the water to the left of the muskrat, and immediately there are no more muskrats to be seen. Charlie touches Dennis's arm: It's all right. They'll be back. We have plenty of time.

Dennis tries several more shots; no luck. He is angry with himself, but Charlie keeps reassuring him. He is handling the gun well. Just as important, he is concealing his frustration. The right opportunity will come if he has patience. Then Grandfather shoots, and soon there are a few dead muskrats in the game bag, almost as many as there were shots fired. They stop to eat. Dennis is disappointed in his luck and getting tired, but he does his best not to show it. After they have rested, they start off again.

Dennis is too anxious now, and when he spots a muskrat he raises his rifle and fires carelessly, missing again. His grandfather shakes his head and begins to tell him a story about the dangers of guns. Dennis is restless—he simply wants a chance to shoot—but he respects his grandfather and listens, anyway. Once there was a man who shot his best friend accidentally when they were out hunting together. The man was so upset by what he had done that he vowed never to hunt again. As a result, two families were poor and without food: the family of the dead man, and the family of the man who would no longer hunt. There have been other cases like that one, but not many. One must be careful.

While they wait, Charlie lectures Dennis about safety.

Dennis does not argue or talk back. Often boys don't agree with their elders' advice, and when they are older they go ahead and do what they want—except when it comes to survival and living off the land. The older generation may not understand the new world, but they know everything there is to know about the old world, and the young men listen to them and accept their experience and wisdom without question.

Soon Dennis's luck improves. They hunt through the sunlit night, and by the time they return to camp early the next morning, Dennis is so exhausted that he can hardly put one foot in front of the other. He sleeps the whole way in the boat, still holding the rifle that is now his. There are fifteen dead muskrats for Liz to skin out, three of them Dennis's. The pelts will bring them a little money, although not as much as the mink and fox from last winter.

The herring are coming. Gulls zoom overhead, shrieking the news, and the surface of the water becomes smooth, a sure sign. The village prepares for action. On their way to spawn, the herring don't stay long—maybe a couple of days, maybe a week—and then they're gone. There's no second chance, and herring is the staple of the winter diet. You have to be ready, Jim says. If you don't get it now, you'll be hungry next winter.

Fortunately most of the men haven't left yet for Dillingham to work on the commercial salmon boats or in the canneries. When they have to leave before the herring run, somebody in the family always has to stay behind to catch herring.

Jim takes David with him in the boat to help with the nets. They anchor one end of the gill net on the bank of the river, and Jim keeps his kicker idling to hold the other end in place. White floats attached along the top edge of the net bob on the surface of the water; the bottom edge is held down with a lead line. The fish, headed upstream and swept in with the tide, are caught by their gills in the mesh of the net.

Jim always goes to the same spot in the river to set his net; he's been doing it for years. David helps him haul the net over the gunwale and into the boat, and they pluck out the slippery, struggling fish and feed out the net again. When the boat is full of fish, they head for shore. David and his father toss the fish into tubs; Judson spells David and goes out onto the river with Jim, and Dennis helps David lug the tubs of fish over to fish racks and dump them into pits lined with grass, where their mother and aunt Julia are waiting. The women cover the pits with a tarp to allow the fish to "work" for a few days, until they're easier to handle.

The first herring to come up the river are the oldest; they are also the fattest and the hardest to dry, and Lucy decides to boil some and store the rest in seal oil. She prefers the next arrivals; they are less oily. But the fishermen play it safe and catch the early ones in case no more come. The last to appear are the youngest fish and the leanest. With luck, by then they've already taken enough to last through the winter and won't need these leathery specimens.

The women work from early morning until late into the night. Lucy grabs a fish in one hand and guts it with two strokes of her thumb. She scoops out the eggs and spreads them to dry. Then Julia takes a blade of rye grass, gathered last fall and dried over the winter, and adds each gutted fish to the long braid she is making. When the braid is a dozen feet long with eighty to a hundred fish strung on it, Adeline and Dennis drape it over a rack built of driftwood. The younger kids have the job of turning the braids several times a day so the fish dry evenly.

In a week of long hours and exhausting labor, the men of the village catch most of the fish they can use next winter—almost two tons to feed a large family. But they take no more than can be used in a season. The dried fish won't keep any longer than that, and tradition keeps them from hoarding.

The women's work of cutting and braiding goes on after the fishing stops, and the racks fill with braids of fish. At first the weather is blustery and damp, and Lucy's hands ache with the cold. One morning it starts to rain, and they rush around throwing tarps over the racks to protect the drying fish. They worry; wet weather can keep the fish from drying and the whole catch could turn moldy. But they keep on gutting and braiding.

But after a few days the sun breaks through, and the sisters laugh and chat in its warmth. By the end of the month the fish are dry, and they pull them from the braids and store them in baskets. The fish that recently glittered in the river have become part of next winter's food supply. But there's no time to rest; the salmon have started to run.

Alice is tearful. Tomorrow is the day Judson leaves for Dillingham on Bristol Bay, about 250 miles south of Chaputnguak, where he will work at one of the salmon canneries. He tries to console her: he may be gone for only a few weeks, depending on the catch. Last year the season was poor, and the men worked less than two weeks. On the other hand, he might be gone for a couple of months—and he needs the money for college.

The rivers and creeks, lakes and ponds of the tundra teem with fish and water life. The mighty king salmon, or chinook, have begun their struggle upstream to the headwaters of the rivers to spawn. When they leave the ocean they are strong and weigh as much as sixty pounds, some even more, but the fight against the current for hundreds of miles exhausts them. Once in the headwaters they lay their eggs and die, their life cycle complete; the young salmon hatch and swim down to the sea. Some of them live for as long as nine years, feeding on the ocean floor before they return to their own river to spawn.

The chinook swim near the riverbanks, avoiding the

main force of the current and resting in the eddies. In these shallow eddies where the current swirls back on itself, the Yup'iks set their nets, checking them twice a day to collect the salmon and other ocean fish that have been caught there. At about the same time the smaller red salmon, or sockeye, are spawning in the lakes. By the end of the month the chum salmon, still smaller and less oily and therefore easier to dry, are on their way. In the old days chums were fed to the dog teams; some people still call them "dog salmon."

Salmon fishing has long been big business in Alaska. The men leave for Bristol Bay or Bethel to work on commercial fishing boats or in the canneries that buy the catch. When Jim Koonuk sees Judson and the others off at the airstrip, he remembers when he spent summers with his uncle David, the captain of a large fishing boat. It was a big, expensive vessel with hydraulically operated nets for hauling in the salmon. As captain, Uncle David was able to pick his own crew, and naturally he had taken Jim along. But now all that has changed. After Uncle David was killed in an accident, his son Jack inherited the boat and also the permit required for commercial fishing. But Jack had an alcohol problem, and he sold the permit for ten thousand dollars. Today, that permit would be worth at least three hundred thousand dollars, maybe more. It makes Jim sick to think what happened to it.

When the Alaska Fish and Game Commission started issuing permits in the 1970s, the idea was to keep the area from being overfished. The Yup'iks respect the philosophy, but people like Jim wonder how it has happened that most of those permits are no longer in the hands of Native Alaskans but have been bought up by big fishing companies from Outside. And young men like Judson will put in a few weeks of grueling work in order to earn a few thousand dollars, the only chance most of the villagers have to bring home some cash.

The salmon run on the Kuskokwim, too, but not in such huge numbers as they did before commercial fishing became a major industry in the 1960s. In the old days, entire village populations moved to fish camp in the summer. It was a chance to visit with friends and relatives from other villages and to share both the work and the results of it. There are still a number of fish camps along the Kuskokwim, and Charlie and Liz Koonuk have packed up their younger grandchildren and taken their boat to her brother's fish camp near Bethel. Liz's family has been camping at the same spot along the river for several generations, and one of the reasons for going is that the children enjoy it so much. So do the adults—it's good to get away from the closeness of the village, even if it means a lot of work.

Today the harvests are far larger down around Bristol Bay and up on the Yukon, and the fish there are oilier and considered better quality by the buyers. Still, in an effort to make sure the river is not fished out, Fish and Game has issued permits on the Kuskokwim, too, allowing commer-

Commercial salmon fishing on the major rivers of Alaska draws young people to work on the processors and in the canneries.

cial boats to fish only during certain periods. They sell to the processors in Bethel—sockeye fetches the highest prices, king is next in value, and "dog salmon" is at the bottom.

While many of the men have left the village to fish for money, those who stay behind fish for the winter's food. Jim and David empty the gill nets of salmon, and Lucy and her sister-in-law, Julia, prepare their *uluaqs* for the day's catch. Cutting salmon properly for drying is an art; the cuts must be positioned just so, at a precise angle, of a certain depth. If it's not done right, the salmon doesn't dry properly, or it gets wormy. David helps to lug tubs of fish from his father's boat to where they're working. Lucy scales the fish, slits it open, and throws the innards in a bucket. Then she passes the cleaned fish to Julia, who deftly fillets it, leaving the pieces connected at the tail to hang over the fish rack. All around the village women squat for hours, working steadily until the pile of fresh fish is gone and the racks outside each house are crowded with salmon hung up to dry.

In other parts of the United States June 22, the summer solstice, marks the first day of summer, the day with the most hours of daylight. But in Chaputnguak and elsewhere in the Arctic, the days of summer are literally endless. For a few weeks before and after the solstice, the sun does not set; it merely slips toward the sea, rolls along the northern horizon on the far side of the Urrsukvaaq River, and then climbs the sky again. The continuous daylight seems to make people more active, less inclined to sleep. Often the children are playing outside until midnight or later; they go to bed for a few hours and then rush outside again.

The weather is not particularly warm; although the sun is bright and hot, a chilling wind blows continually. Most people wear sweaters or jackets, but the children run barefoot. They seem to be always covered with mud.

Their work finished, the women gather along the boardwalk and watch the late evening sun shimmer on the pond and cast long shadows on the tundra. They talk quietly, aware of the many sounds around them. The air whirs with the wingbeats of geese, ducks, gulls, terns, and ptarmigans. Shouts drift from the wooden deck outside the school, where the younger boys shoot hoops.

Alice comes by to talk to Lucy and Adeline; she's missing Judson and wants to find out if they've heard from him, but she doesn't ask directly. Patiently she works the conversation around in his direction and learns that they have not. Talking to his family just makes her miss him even more.

Old men come out of the steam baths, their wrinkled skin shiny with sweat, and sit naked on the grass to cool off. No one goes to bed before midnight. Time enough to sleep in the long, dark winter.

CHAPTER 10

July

Pauline Egoak could not be more thrilled. For her birthday her brother Larry gave her a round-trip ticket to Bethel, and she has made plans to fly there over the Fourth of July, to visit friends and also to stop around at the AC and Swanson's, the town's two major supermarket–department stores, to see if there are any job openings. One more thing: she's heard that Sam Michael, her once-upon-a-time boyfriend, is working at the fish-processing plant in Bethel this summer. She's hoping to run into him accidentally on purpose.

The tundra wears its summer blanket of flowers, but Pauline isn't much interested in scenic beauty during the one-hour flight. The moment her bag arrives on the conveyor belt in the small terminal, she rushes outside and with four other passengers piles into a taxi headed for town.

On the local map, Bethel is centrally located, halfway

Bethel is the hub of bush Alaska and attracts people from dozens of small villages for business and pleasure.

between Anchorage and Russia, and seven hundred miles south of Point Barrow on the Arctic Ocean. With a population of about 4,500, Bethel is the unofficial capital of a seventy thousand-square-mile chunk of southwestern Alaska, the place where jets from Anchorage land and barges from Seattle unload, where villagers come to shop, see the doctor, and visit family and friends, where Yup'ik values often run up against *kass'aq* ways.

People have always congregated in Bethel, many of them—like Pauline—looking for work. But *kass'aqs* from the Outside usually take the scarce jobs, and subsistence resources in the area are not enough to support the transplanted villagers. Those who do move in from the villages and find work send money home, and the folks at home send them the wild foods that can no longer be found around Bethel. In one of the bags that Pauline crams into the taxi for the ride to her friend Emily's is a package of herring and a container of greens put up in seal oil by Emily's mother.

According to legend, a young couple fleeing famine on the Yukon rested by the Kuskokwim, found their fish traps full in the morning, and decided to stay. The Yup'ik settlement was called *Mamterillermiut,* "people of many fish caches." The Moravian missionaries who arrived in 1884 liked the location, too—it was close to a couple of other villages and to a trading post—and decided to build their mission across the river from the settlement. That day they read in their Bible, "And God said unto Jacob, Arise, go up to Bethel, and dwell there; and make there an altar unto God, that appeared unto thee when thou fleddest from the face of Esau thy brother." And so they named their mission Bethel, meaning "house of God."

There is another, less pleasant legend about the place. In it the missionaries were warned by a shaman who prophesied that the new mission would fall into the river. And much of it has; the struggle is ongoing to keep the entire riverfront from washing away as the river changes course. At one time Bethel's junked cars and trucks were piled along the bank, to hold back the forces of erosion. "Bethel Riviera" was partly successful, at least for a while, but environmentalists claimed the hulks leaked oil, and they were hauled away and a new seawall was built, costing the state of Alaska $22 million.

By the mid-1960s, Bethel had earned a terrible reputation: one of the highest poverty levels in the United States, with out-of-control problems of alcoholism, crime, and suicide. In 1984 there were more murders in Bethel, population then about four thousand, than in Anchorage, population four hundred thousand. "House of God" was called by some "the armpit of Alaska."

Somebody once said that Bethel looks as though it has been laid out by a squirt gun. Dozens of taxis race up and down the few paved roads and the muddy or dusty unpaved ones that wander off toward the tundra. Aboveground arctic water pipe makes it hard to go anywhere in a straight line. There is a handsome new library and cultural center, and one almost suburban-looking neighborhood boasts a few carefully nurtured trees, although no one Pauline knows lives out there—it's strictly *kass'aq*. The water truck delivers twice a week to places not served by the pipe; the "poop truck," replacing the old honey-bucket system, also calls twice a week, for there is still no sewage system. But for Pauline Egoak and other visitors from the bush, Bethel is an exciting place.

On the morning of the Fourth of July the sky is low and overcast, but a light breeze helps to keep the mosquitoes at bay. Pauline and her friends head for Third Avenue to watch the Fourth of July parade of floats and trucks, and then join the throng of people funneling toward Pinky's Park. It's already jammed, although it's still early in the day. The girls work out a plan: if they get separated, they'll meet up again in front of the portable stage. And they're all to keep their eyes open for Sam Michael.

An American flag carried on stage by the color guard whips in the breeze while the national anthem is broadcast over the loudspeakers; the color guard marches off, and a local *kass'aq* noted for his Elvis impersonations takes its place. Next a woman from VISTA—Volunteers in Service to America, a government program—demonstrates all kinds of imaginative ways to recycle old plastic sacks; she's even made a hat from them.

The girls wander away from the stage past rows and rows of concession booths selling chili dogs and soft drinks and raffle tickets. There are chances to win aluminum boats and outboard motors and guns and all sorts of other prizes, including cash—the biggest is ten thousand dollars. Pauline buys one chance on a pair of round-trip airplane tickets to Hawaii and another on a Ford pickup. Emily teases her; what good is it to buy only one ticket? There are families who are buying them by the fistful, to improve their odds of winning. So Emily buys a ticket for the Hawaii prize and the pickup as well, and they agree to share if they win, although they're not sure how they'd share the truck. Several times during the day they go back to the booths and buy more tickets, to improve the odds.

Children enjoy an unusual treat at a village Fourth of July celebration.

Back in Chaputnguak, the Fourth of July will get under way as soon as somebody gets around to organizing it. Pauline's brother Larry is the logical person to do the organizing. For one thing, he's a member of the village council and has official status; for another, he's one of the few younger men in town at this time of year; for a third, he and his father own the village store. The council has allotted money to be used for prizes—lots of candy bars and Cracker Jacks so that each child will get something, and soap, hand cream, paper towels, tobacco and such for the adults, which Larry will provide to the council at his wholesale cost, in addition to the cash prizes. There will also be plenty of soft drinks for everybody and dozens of oranges to give away.

In the villages this strictly American holiday is traditionally a day for races and games with prizes and free treats. Many of the contests have their roots in competitions that once took place in the *qasgiq,* which served as a kind of gymnasium where young people competed in sports. Many of the men's contests had to do with strength and agility, skills needed by hunters. There were tests of finger strength, for instance, and arm, leg, and neck strength. In the standing kick, the contestant leaped up to kick a seal bladder suspended overhead. After each try, the bladder was raised higher; to qualify, both feet had to hit it together. The standing kick is still an athletic specialty of many young Yup'ik men, but the bladder has been replaced by a large rubber ball.

Sometimes the women's contests were held in the *qasgiq.* Many tested their ability to escape from pursuing men. But the women who race down the Chaputnguak airstrip on this Fourth of July are not practicing a getaway from unwanted suitors; they just like to run. One of the favorite Fourth of July contests is the old women's footrace, in which they prove that although they may carry many years on their backs, their legs are still strong and fast.

There was a time when games were played without the pressure to win that exists today. The point of most games and contests was not so much to beat someone else but to beat one's own personal score. When the *kass'aq* teachers first introduced football, for example, the children enjoyed

A village elder judges a contestant's performance of the standing kick.

kicking the ball around, but they cheered for one another rather than forming teams. They've changed traditional American baseball to suit their own ideas, too, getting a player out by hitting him with the ball as he runs the bases.

In the old days most Yup'ik children had homemade toys, but today toys are bought at one of the stores in Bethel or ordered from catalogs. A traditional toy called "Eskimo yo-yo" by *kass'aqs* is still made by some village women for the tourist trade: two small balls of sealskin are attached to the ends of a leather thong. The child holds the thong just off the center and starts one ball circling in front of her. Then she starts the second ball circling in the opposite direction. By an easy motion of her wrist, she can keep the two balls going for as long as she likes.

It's about ten o'clock when everyone begins to gather between the school and the airstrip for the Fourth of July contests. There will be no standing kick—the young men who do it so well are all away working—but there is race after race, for different ages and different sexes. The winner of the old women's footrace is a favorite grandmother who wins nearly every year, and her victory is greeted by cheers. The children run, the old men run. Mothers line up their toddlers, and the kids lurch toward a sister or grandmother at the finish line. Next the older boys and girls choose sides for a tug-of-war that always ends with one side or the other wallowing in the mud.

The women take their turn at tug-of-war, cheered on by the men and children.

This year the council voted to have a dinner at the community center, and late in the afternoon each family takes food to the hall. There is free soda, and Larry has ordered frozen pizza and watermelon and *kass'aq* ice cream, flown in from the AC in Bethel. When the meal is over, no one is in a hurry to go home. The adults talk and watch as the children skip stones over the smooth water of the pond. The day went well; people obviously enjoyed themselves. It was a bang-up Fourth of July—maybe the best ever in Chaputnguak.

At the end of the day in Bethel when the winning tickets are drawn, Pauline and Emily haven't won a thing. They've spent far more than they'd intended—on nothing. But worse, much much worse, is the fact that Pauline finally spotted Sam in the crowd, Sam for whom she has been yearning for months. But he didn't see her. He was too busy with another girl.

What the Fourth of July is *not,* anywhere in village Alaska, is a celebration of American freedom and independence. Yup'ik children are taught American history in school, of course. They recognize the names of George Washington and the other Founding Fathers. They have heard stories about Betsy Ross, the Liberty Bell, Paul Revere, the Declaration of Independence, the American

Revolution, the Civil War. But for most of the children, American history is as remote as the study of African geography.

And so, except in Bethel with the playing of "The Star-Spangled Banner" and the marching of the color guard, there was no patriotic observance of the day. The Fourth of July in its true meaning has nothing to do with Yup'ik Eskimos, and the history of the United States seems to touch them in only the most remote ways.

Being represented by one of the stars on the miniature flag on the post office counter does not mean much to Yup'iks living in Chaputnguak or any other isolated village in the bush. Their contact with the government is through agencies that do things for their family: The state of Alaska instructs their children; the Public Health Service treats diseases that were introduced by the *kass'aqs* in the first place; welfare agencies and food stamp programs help to feed them. Or their contact is through agencies that seem to work against them: federal laws prohibit them from shooting the food they need when they need it; state laws dictate when and how many fish they can catch and sell; the state housing authority has given them poor homes unsuitable for the harsh climate; and federal housing laws don't allocate enough money to provide sanitation and safe water.

In 1971 Congress passed the Alaska Native Land Claims Settlement Act, turning over to the Native Alaskans title to 44 million acres of land and nearly a billion dollars in federal funds and mineral rights. To handle all this money, Alaska was divided into thirteen regional corporations, each with an elected board of directors. Each region is made up of village corporations, one for each village with at least twenty-five residents. Bethel belongs to the regional corporation called Calista (pronounced cha-LIS-ta and meaning "our thing"), which includes over a quarter of the villages in Alaska, far more than any other region. In the 1990 census, there were 19,447 people in the forty-nine villages.

But the money has gradually leaked away, and there is little left for villages to build new community projects or to maintain old ones. The average income in Calista is the lowest in the state, and the birth rate is the highest, almost double the national rate. There are lots of village children who will graduate without a good chance of finding a job.

Young people like Pauline are beginning to move out of the villages to urban areas, looking for work. But most of them lack job skills or education to get the better-paying jobs, even in Bethel. The young men leave, but they don't have know-how or self-confidence, they find themselves far from their families, friends, culture, and community, and most of them wind up going home again.

The odds are improving for Pauline, though: the day after the Fourth she stops by the AC and speaks to the manager, asking if there are any openings. As it happens, he remembers when she was in the training program two years ago. She made a good impression on him, and he promises to give her a chance. She can begin stocking shelves the very next day, if she wants. And she does, she does!

But back at Emily's she begins to weep. "Homesick already?" Emily asks, and Pauline nods.

Summer is tourist season in many parts of Alaska, and white visitors pour into the state from all over the country. Some drive all the way from the Lower Forty-eight on the Alaska Highway. Once in Alaska, though, they can't go far on wheels, because highways do not extend deep into the interior. (There are fewer highway miles in Alaska than in the relatively tiny state of Vermont.) Many people cruise by ship through the islands of the Alexander Archipelago in Southeastern. Thousands visit Denali National Park, to see or climb Mount McKinley, the highest peak in North America. People come in droves to hunt and fish; so do hikers and campers and others who love the pristine wilderness. But only a few ever visit coastal Alaska to admire the spectacular colors of the tundra.

All encounter the summer siege of mosquitoes. Visitors go home with tales of mosquitoes in clouds so thick they obscure your vision, invade your mouth and nose, drop into your food. The trick is to ignore them, as the Yup'iks do. Mosquitoes are an important part of the ecology in this area, a national wildlife refuge and one of the most important bird breeding grounds of the continent. The insects' life cycle corresponds with the life of the birds that have just hatched and need huge quantities of them for food. When the nestlings are on their own, the mosquito season ends.

The children aren't much bothered by mosquitoes. Katie catches them by the handful to feed her pet baby gull. Grandmother Liz brought her the gull egg, and for weeks Katie kept it warm near the kitchen stove. One day recently she heard a tapping sound, and within a few hours the shell broke open and the little gull stuck out its fuzzy head. Dennis used to hatch a gull each summer for a pet, but something always happened to it: a dog got it, or one of the children accidentally brought it down with a sling-shot, or it flew away. But Katie is delighted with the fluffy little bird that she can hold in her two hands. She takes it out to show her friends who are playing on the boardwalk and to catch its supper.

In a few short weeks the chill north winds will begin to blow across the tundra, but for now the villagers of all ages want to enjoy every hour of warmth and daylight. It is past midnight when the children stop their play and their mothers call them inside for a few hours of sleep.

CHAPTER 11

August

Judson has been back from Bristol Bay for a couple of weeks. It was a good season, and he piled up quite a bit of money—saved nearly all of it, too, until the end. He stayed away from the bunk room poker games, where a lot of cash changed hands, and although he met boys and girls his own age, he didn't go out with them much. Then, when he was ready to leave for home, his friends Eddie and Steve got the idea of stopping off in Anchorage for a few days to see the sights. Eddie said they could stay with his relatives and eat with them, too—they wouldn't have to spend much at all. It was a temptation Judson couldn't resist. Wallet bulging with more cash than he had ever seen at one time, he flew to Anchorage.

With an area population of over four hundred

thousand, the city is a sprawling checkerboard laid out on the flat plain between the majestic Chugach Mountains and Cook Inlet, an arm of the Pacific Ocean. Originally settled by whites and for a long time almost exclusively a *kass'aq* city, Anchorage is the largest Native Alaskan settlement in the state, with Fairbanks running second.

Judson's friend Eddie, who has been to Anchorage three or four times and regards himself as an old hand at city life, plans to come to live in the city when he finishes job training in Bethel and will get a job doing some kind of electronics work. Someday, he says, he'll live in a fine apartment and own a car and stroll down Fourth Avenue every night.

This is a popular dream among village people, and many of them try it. They go to Anchorage or Fairbanks, where jobs are scarce, and often find themselves living in poor ghettos under worse conditions than they ever experienced in the bush. Sometimes they go Outside and work in Seattle on fishing boats or get factory jobs in Chicago or Detroit. But noise, traffic, and crowds get the best of them, and they dislike the climate and the fast pace and pressure to watch the clock. They get homesick and return to their villages again. Unable to adapt to the rigors of subsistence hunting and fishing, many of them wind up collecting welfare.

Judson had been to Anchorage a couple of times on student trips, but a teacher always went along. This was much more exciting. The first day he and his friends hung around Fourth Avenue, the neon-lit midtown strip that lures most village Alaskans who come to the big city for a good time. That evening they took a taxi to the home of Eddie's relatives in a low-income housing project. They sat on the floor in the crowded apartment and ate smoked fish that had been sent to the Anchorage Yup'iks by family in the bush.

The next day they went back to Fourth Avenue, this time to the other end, where hundreds of well-dressed *kass'aq* tourists emerged from the modern high-rise hotels to browse in the souvenir shops. In a store window Eddie saw baskets like the ones his mother, Josephine, makes, with eye-popping price tags: three hundred dollars, some of them even more—twice as much as she gets from the dealer. Why did the store get so much and his mother so little? Eddie wondered. Judson shrugged; he didn't know, either.

Judson wanted to see more of the city, and he thought of getting on one of the city buses just to see where it went. But he had never been on a bus, and he was afraid of ending up lost. It was one thing to be out on the tundra alone in a winter storm with whiteness in every direction, but several lanes of cars, traffic lights, and a bus headed who-knew-where among the huge buildings and endless streets were something else. He decided not to try.

By now ravenously hungry, the boys wandered from

cheap diner to fast-food shop, peering in the windows until they found a restaurant that looked inviting and dared each other to go inside. The hostess seated them in a booth and presented them with menus. This was a lot better than the Korean place in Bethel, the only restaurant Judson had ever been in. They paged through the menu featuring photographs of colorful meals. His friends didn't want to spend much money, but this was not an obstacle: Judson offered to pay for everything.

So they started with ham and eggs and pancakes and French toast, continued with hamburger platters heaped with fries, grilled steak with baked potatoes, and baskets of fried chicken, and ended with two kinds of pie plus chocolate brownies topped with ice cream. "Are you sure?" the waitress asked warily. "It's a lot of food."

They were sure. They were men, and they were hungry. The manager stopped by and told them they'd have to pay up after each round of food. Judson flashed his roll of bills and agreed.

Plate after plate arrived, and they did their best, although toward the end they were barely tasting what was brought. Judson didn't know how to stop the parade of food. People stared, and Judson was embarrassed. When he'd paid the final check, Judson realized that the feast had cost him over two hundred dollars. Nobody had told him about tipping, so of course he didn't leave one.

That night Eddie bought a bottle of whiskey to

celebrate the end of the visit, and Judson got drunk for the first time in his life. The next day he boarded the jet to Bethel; a few hours later he crawled out of the cramped seat of a plane in Chaputnguak, bewildered, exhausted, and hung over.

Homecoming was a relief. While Alice and his family clustered around him, Judson distributed the gifts he had bought: a plate with a painting of Mount McKinley for Lucy, a silk scarf featuring the state flower, forget-me-not, for Alice, a leather wallet for Jim, T-shirts for his brothers and sisters. He would do almost anything to avoid telling his father about the extravagant feast. They'd been counting on that money for college expenses.

Happy as they were to see Judson again, there was a touch of sadness to this homecoming, because they all know he won't be there for long. At the end of the month he will leave for technical school in Seattle. Judson is excited and also very nervous. Anchorage was overwhelming; what's Seattle going to be like? And so far away, so different from everything he knows.

Soon the fall weather will sweep down—cold, rainy, windy—and people will spend more time indoors. But now everyone is outside as much as possible. David and Dennis take their father's boat to collect driftwood near the mouth of the river. Driftwood is valuable for so many things: big pieces for building projects, small ones for fuel in the steam baths.

A boy collects driftwood to use as fuel in his family's steam bath.

And it's berry season. Women from grandmothers to little girls scour the tundra nearly every day, hunting for berries. A combination of sun, rain, and temperature determine the number and sweetness of the berries to be picked. First to ripen are the orange-red salmonberries, hard to gather because they're scattered and you have to keep moving to reach them. Next come blueberries and cranberries that grow more densely, so that the picker can kneel or squat in one place for a while.

Katie goes foraging with Lucy or Adeline and proudly fills her coffee can. She's not much tempted to eat the berries instead of dropping them in the can, because

Generations of Yup'ik women and children have scoured the tundra in early fall for berries to make *akutaq* or to preserve for winter.

they are very sour. As the cans fill up, the children take them to their older relatives and dump them into the bigger containers. At home they'll eat the berries fresh in *akutaq* or store them in barrels with seal oil as a preservative or put them in freezers. Berry picking sometimes involves the whole family, going by boat to favorite picking grounds and coming back with several barrels full of berries. A family needs about a hundred pounds of berries as part of the winter diet.

The recipe for *akutaq* varies; in some places pressed whitefish and greens are mixed with berries and seal oil or with reindeer tallow, but in Chaputnguak *akutaq* is mostly a mixture of berries and Crisco with sugar. Liz Koonuk adds instant mashed potatoes to hers; Lucy doesn't, but both believe you need to eat *akutaq* to stay warm. And certainly you need the vitamin C that berries provide, far more than you get from the same amount of citrus fruits.

One of the major events of August is the arrival of the barge with basic supplies for the coming year. Dennis and his friends are the first to spot it, and they run back to the village with the news. All the able-bodied males are enlisted to help with the unloading, and a crowd of spectators gathers to watch the goods come off: An aluminum boat for one of the men in the village. A load of lumber to replace part of the boardwalk. Cartons of merchandise for Egoak's store. Crates containing snow machines, four-wheelers, outboard motors, television sets.

Lucy is watching for the box with the blue velvet sofa with tufted cushions and a silky fringe around the bottom. It is something she has wanted for a long time, and last winter Jim told her to go ahead and order it. In the old days people usually sat on the floor; many of the old women still prefer to sit with their legs stuck straight out in front of them while they sew or work on their skins or baskets. But television, magazines, and mail-order catalogs have introduced *kass'aq* ideas of decorating, taking the Yup'iks a long way from the simplicity of the sod house with its few furnishings. For a long time Lucy's visitors will probably avoid her sofa because of its awesome newness. But it represents status for Lucy: her husband has a job that allows him to buy such luxuries. The old couch will be passed on to Jim's sister Anna, whose house always looks as though a storm has blown through it.

Early in the month Jim spent a few days in Bethel for a workshop on school cooking. Now he's on hand to supervise the delivery of supplies for the school kitchen: paper napkins, canned applesauce, peanut butter, powdered milk, cocoa mix, pudding mix, and so on that will be used to feed 110 students for the coming year; fresh items will be flown in as needed. Walter and Marcia Prescott are back from their home in Arizona, and Walter is checking off cartons of books, paper and pencils, art supplies, a video camera, and some new basketballs. Marcia watches over their personal order of staples—flour, sugar, coffee, rice. She'll order meat, cheese, and other perishable foods by mail.

But probably the most critical item to come by barge is the winter supply of fuel oil. Jim remembers when it was his task to clean out the thirty fifty-five-gallon drums that belonged to his family, to roll them up to the barge to be filled, and then to haul them away to be stored. Now the village corporation buys the winter's supply, stores it in three massive yellow tanks on the edge of the village, and sells it to customers as they need it. People used to worry that they hadn't bought enough, that the winter would be fiercer than usual and they'd use up all their fuel before warm weather—the only option was to have it flown in. It's easier now, with the big storage tanks, but oil is still a family's biggest expense, about $3,600 a year to warm a small house.

In a few days the rest of the teachers will come back from their summer leave, signaling the end of long days of freedom. Tommy is excited—he'll enter kindergarten. His sisters are happy for school to start again. David now becomes a ninth-grader—senior high!—which is okay, but other things are more important. There's the possibility of having Judson's room, now that Judson is about to leave for Seattle. There's the possibility that his father or his uncle or his grandfather will take him along for fall seal hunting. And one more thing: Judson has agreed to let David use the beautiful rifle he got for Christmas.

The night before Judson and several other students leave, the village council sponsors a farewell party. It's a time of intensely mixed emotions. Parents whose sons and daughters are leaving for the first time are most upset, because they aren't sure how their children will react to the outside world. Maybe they'll change too much and won't want to come home again. Maybe they won't change enough, and they'll be miserable and homesick. It's a good thing, this chance for an education, the parents tell each other and their children. But inside they're miserable, and the young people are full of anxiety.

The evening begins with a supper in the community hall, a last chance to enjoy wild foods before the students go out to *kass'aq* cooking. Afterward the older folks and little kids go home, and an all-night party gets under way for the teenagers. Somebody hooks up a couple of amplifiers to the stereo system, and rock music blasts across the silent tundra. It goes on without a pause. No one can get any sleep, but there are no complaints: it's for the young people, it's their last night, let them enjoy themselves. Separate groups of boys and girls stand together, lean against the walls, watch the other groups. Not many actually dance.

Empty soft drink cans and a few beer cans clatter into

cartons. Many of the high school students have begun to drink, despite the warnings of their elders. No one is quite sure how the beer got into Chaputnguak, though, given the village ban against any kind of alcohol. It doesn't take much beer to have an effect on the young people, and a few of them are obviously and loudly intoxicated. Some marijuana has been smuggled in, too. Judson was offered joints freely in Dillingham and in Anchorage, but given the "zero tolerance" rule on drugs, he's always a little surprised to see it here in the village.

Drugs and beer don't tempt him, though; not tonight. A few couples, including Alice and Judson, drift out into the darkness—it lasts for a few hours now—and a chance to be alone. He promises to write; she promises to write. They discuss again the hope that they'll be together someday, but in the meantime, they're free to make friends with other people. She cries; he tries not to.

Judson's plane is to leave late in the morning, and the farewells grow more intense. Lucy is weeping openly. She hugs him over and over, reminding him to take care of himself, to be good, to study hard, to come home soon. Jim doesn't cry, but his face is deeply furrowed. He shakes hands with Judson, looks away, shoves his hands deep in his pants pocket. David is the brave one, the oldest son at home, the heir to Judson's little bedroom, the custodian of his rifle.

Alice is there, too, eyes red and swollen.

Finally Judson's belongings are loaded, he climbs

on board with the other passengers, and the plane lumbers slowly to the end of the runway. The engines roar; they lift off fast. Everyone on the ground waves, and some wipe their eyes with their sleeves. Alice's friends gather around to comfort her. The plane banks sharply and levels off again, and to the passengers the tiny village appears below as a cluster of matchboxes. Judson has an unswallowable lump in his throat. He refuses to look back.

CHAPTER 12

September

Long hair scooped back with pink barrettes, Katie dawdles, giggles, and skips her way to school with Agnes and their friend Tina. Dennis walks with Tina's brother, Raymond, passing a ball back and forth. Katie and Tina are in third grade this year and Agnes is in fourth; the girls are all in the same room with the same teacher, a *kass'aq* named Susan Edwards. Susan has long blond hair that she fixes in a variety of clever ways, and the girls are hoping she'll teach them how to do a French braid. Susan also wears nail polish, and they plan to ask her someday to let them try it.

Susan and her husband, Ted, who teaches earth science and math, live in the teachers' quarters in the old Bureau of Indian Affairs school, next door to Walter and Marcia. Susan is very nice, but she is young and inexperienced in teaching in the bush. She's always trying to rush them: "Hurry hurry hurry," she says. "I'll give you one minute to take your seats," and starts counting down in fifteen-second intervals.

Susan writes on the board, "Cinderella wanted to . . ." and the children take out their journals. Katie dislikes the writing exercises, so she wanders slowly around the classroom, getting a tissue, blowing her nose, stopping to admire Tina's Betty Boop T-shirt, meandering back to her desk, anything but writing. Agnes tries to work on the assignment, but she doesn't know how to spell the words she wants to use. Every other minute she pops up to ask Darlene, the aide, for help: "How do you spell animal?" "How do you spell journey?"

"Time's up!" Susan says, and whisks them to the gym for PE. Energetically she runs laps with them, takes them through twenty jumping jacks, ten push-ups, and some stretching exercises. Next she organizes them into teams to play a furious form of soccer.

Back in the classroom for ESL, English as a Second Language, Susan shows them a colored poster with an urban scene. "You can tell it's a city because of the buildings and paved roads." Together they identify library, post office, police station, supermarket, traffic light, bank, fire station, and gas station and compare it to their village, Yes, there's a post office in Chaputnguak, but the library is in the school, and you couldn't really say that Egoak's store is a supermarket, and you can't actually call a police station the shack where the VPSOs occasionally lock up somebody until one of the three Alaska state troopers assigned to the area flies out. There is no bank, nor is there a gas station, unless you count Egoak's, where the men buy gas for their kickers and snow machines. Neither is there a fire department—and that can mean tragedy when one of the wooden buildings catches fire, as St. Cecilia's did a few years ago and burned all the way to the ground and there was nothing anyone could do.

Then Susan hands out a map of the scene they've been discussing and tells them to label the buildings, starting with the post office in the center of town. She reads the directions: "The library is to the right of the post office. The supermarket is in front of the library. The police station is to the left of the supermarket. The fire station is in back of the library." But Katie loses track: "How can this be?" she asks, and gives up and goes to see how Agnes is doing.

"You don't have much time until lunch," Susan warns them. "Hurry hurry hurry."

Nobody seems to be paying attention. Susan touches her nose and the top of her head and says, "All those who have their eyes on me, do this." But not many have their eyes on her, and there's not much response. Katie is busy getting a book from the shelf for reading period, *Ma and Pa Dracula* by Ann M. Martin.

After lunch Susan opens the "ticket store." All week

she has been handing out tickets for good behavior, and once a week she lets them trade them in for trinkets. Katie has her eye on a tiny paper Japanese fan, but her classroom wandering has gotten her in trouble a few times, and she doesn't have nearly enough tickets. No problem—Tina has a fistful, and she shares them with Katie. Brought up in a society that emphasizes sharing, the kids are always giving their tickets to their friends; Susan tries to stop this practice, but it's a losing battle.

Then it's time to work on days and dates. "What will be tomorrow's date?" she asks. Tina goes to the board and carefully prints the answer—but Agnes can see that it's turning out wrong, and she runs up to the board to help her. Tina quickly erases the error with her fingers, and the students remind Tina in a chorus, "Not with your hand!" It's another one of Susan's rules.

Next they work with nickels, dimes, quarters, and pennies, real ones from Susan's purse, in order to figure out how many of each you need to add up to a certain amount. Katie gets bored. She sneaks *Ma and Pa Dracula* out of her desk and, keeping the book out of sight on her lap, reads another couple of pages.

For Dennis not much has changed: the same teacher, Catherine Tom, the same big room with the fifth grade. Adeline has moved over to Jerry Waterman's seventh- and eighth-grade room. David has assured her that Jerry is really a good guy. David himself is now on the other side of the building, with the senior high students. Instead of staying in the same room with the same teacher all day, he follows a complicated schedule. Monday is divided into eight periods, the rest of the week into four periods each day, with different rooms for different subjects, taught by different teachers.

David has Marcia Prescott for English language development and Walter for general math; then Susan's husband, Ted Edwards, for earth science, and Leon Wassilie for Yup'ik, a computer class taught by Walter, and a study skills class with Marcia again. No two days are exactly alike. David thinks he's never going to get it figured out; the only thing that stays the same is lunch.

The work seems harder, and there's more of it. In the evenings David goes back to the school to do his homework in the library from seven to eight-thirty. But that's just marking time until the gym opens and he can shoot hoops until 10:00 P.M.—about all there is to do in the evenings in Chaputnguak. The church opens its recreation center, really just a Ping-Pong table and a few tattered magazines, on Monday and Wednesday evenings for kids through eighth grade, and on Tuesday and Thursday for high school students. There's a curfew during the week—9:00 P.M. for younger kids, 10:00 P.M. for high school students—but part of the fun is ducking the VPSO who patrols the village enforcing it.

It took David a few days to realize how much he'd miss Judson. He thinks a lot about Judson, wondering how he's doing in Seattle. He personally cannot imagine such a thing, being so far away, especially now that his father has promised to take him seal hunting on the next good weekend.

What he'd really like to do—but can't ask—is to go moose hunting with his mother's cousin Larry and some other men from the village. There are no moose out here on the coast—they range in the forested inland regions—but every fall when Fish and Game allows a moose hunt, Larry drives his powerful boat all the way up the Kuskokwim River to the hunting grounds. There is no room in the boat for a boy who has not yet gotten his first seal.

It could happen this fall, though. The seals have come back to the mouths of the rivers, and the men hunt them in open water as long as they can get the boats out before freeze-up. These aren't the best seals: these are the ringed and spotted seals, smaller than the big bearded seals, their layers of fat are gone, and there aren't nearly as many of them as there were in the spring. But he's going hunting, and that's what matters.

When the weekend finally arrives, David is naturally excited and naturally tries not to show it. He nervously fingers Judson's rifle, and he does manage to get off a couple of good shots when his father gives him permission, but nobody is having much luck: the thin seals sink before the hunters can get to them.

Then, just as they're about to head home with only a

couple of puny seals shot by somebody else to show for the day's hunting, an amazing thing happens: Jim stands up in the boat and points to a huge white object in the water—a beluga whale.

The chase begins. Sometimes the whale dives, disappearing with a dramatic flash of its enormous flukes, and then it surfaces again. The men maneuver the boats this way and that, and finally manage to head the whale toward shallow water. Jim quietly reaches for Judson's rifle, more powerful than his own, and David hands it over without protest. It is Jim's well-placed shot that makes the kill.

They tie the beast between two boats and slowly tow it to a beach near the mouth of the river. One of the older men known to be the best butcher goes to work on it, first cutting away strips of blubber and then carving out chunks of meat. Jim is given the choicest cuts, including the liver; the other hunters get their shares; the rest will be distributed to families in the village. Almost every part of the whale is taken; David shyly asks for one of the teeth. He wants to give it to his brother Dennis, who has shown an interest in carving.

The beluga whale was a lucky break for the subsistence hunters, but the main emphasis is still on fish. Dennis has promised Grandfather Charlie he'll help him put his blackfish trap at the mouth of the pond. Charlie wove his funnel-shaped trap with strips of driftwood—a complex craft that many of the younger men haven't learned; newer traps are made of wire mesh. They set the trap with its mouth upstream and leave a marker to show where it is even after the streams are covered with a foot of ice and deep snow has fallen. Every few days they'll open the hole in the ice, lift out the trap and empty the fish, put the trap back in the water, and throw chipped ice in the hole to help it freeze over faster. For the next couple of months while the blackfish are running, Dennis's mother and grandmother will serve it boiled and freeze some to eat later, dipped raw in seal oil.

Toward the end of September the temperatures drop into the thirties at night, and the berry picking and greens gathering slow down. After the first frost Adeline goes with her friend Rose and Rose's mother, Josephine, to pick fine, supple blades of rye grass one at a time for making baskets and for braiding fish. In the old days gathering grass was a big job in the fall; bales of grass were needed to make insoles for mukluks. Only a few women still sew sealskin boots. Gathering grass is now a more leisurely activity.

Every day Great-grandmother Amelia goes out on the tundra to make ash, just as she does every year at this time. Here and there oil barrels have been laid on their sides and cut open to make stoves. The old women collect the willow branches—or have their grandchildren and great-grandchildren do it for them—stuff them into the

A man checks his fish trap under the ice.

barrels, and slowly burn them to a fine ash, to be mixed with tobacco. It takes about an hour to turn a huge pile of willow branches into a little pile of coals that must be stirred carefully to keep them from blowing away. The job is simple, but it takes a long day of work to produce a five-pound can of ash, enough for one family. Both men and women chew tobacco quids, the object of Walter Prescott's vigorous anti-"chew" campaign.

Amelia patiently waits her turn at a stove, drinking tea and talking with her friends. Amelia has nine living children in the village, and some fifty grandchildren. She has lost count of the number of great-grandchildren, except that one or another of them and sometimes several always come to visit her when she's making ash. She looks across the tundra toward the village and sees one of them—Agnes, is it?—making her way over the uneven ground with another girl, perhaps her sister, and her little brother. Amelia watches them approach. She suddenly feels very tired. It will be nice to have them walk home with her. Then she'll have a nice rest.

Word spreads quickly through the village: Amelia Joe is dead. Amelia was the oldest woman in Chaputnguak, the mother of Liz Koonuk, grandmother of Jim Koonuk, great-grandmother of David, Adeline, Dennis, Agnes, Katie, Tommy, Lilly, and many others. It seems impossible: she was out all day making ash. On the way home she told Agnes and Katie that she felt very tired and she was going to take a nap. She lay down and went to sleep and never woke up.

Everyone in the village has some memory of Amelia: Amelia dressed up in her birdskin parka, made by her own mother. Amelia clutching the yards and yards of inflated seal gut that she used to dry on the clothesline outside her house. Amelia gathering eggs, able to tell the children about every kind of bird in the sky, and how to watch its behavior on the ground so that you could go straight to its nest and collect its eggs. Amelia reminding them to take all the eggs in the nest, to fool the hen into laying another clutch. Amelia finding the "mouse food" hidden by the lemmings. Amelia telling stories—she was the one who passed on some of the stories to Uncle Pete. Amelia, remembering everything about the village, carrying its whole history in her head.

Amelia's daughters, Liz Koonuk and her sisters, perform the task of washing their mother's body and dressing it in the birdskin parka. Some of her belongings are put into the plain plywood coffin with her: the *uluaq* with which she had butchered so many seals, unfinished mukluks on which she had been working, an ivory crucifix. Liz gathers up the rest of her possessions; they will be burned after the funeral. This symbolizes the release of Amelia's soul. Nothing material is passed on to others.

Before the arrival of Christian missionaries, the Yup'iks did not bury their dead but put them in small

Because of the difficulty of digging a grave in the frozen tundra, Yup'iks used to put the corpses of their dead in small driftwood structures.

driftwood houses built on top of the ground. On the outside of the little house they hung the personal belongings of the dead—cooking tools, hunting implements, combs, jewelry. But on the day of Amelia's funeral, half a dozen men of the village take turns digging through the spongy tundra—that's no problem—and into the frozen earth. Then the digging becomes a struggle, but it's easier than when death comes in the winter and they must dig through a couple of feet of ice-packed snow as well. Some of the older couples had gotten together last July and spent a day fixing up the cemetery, straightening and painting the white crosses, mending the fence, arranging plastic flowers on the graves. Someone remembers that Amelia came by that day and teased them: "Are you getting ready for me? I'll be the next one in there!" And sure enough, she is.

That afternoon the men carry the coffin to the church, where the mourners have gathered. Nearly everyone in town is present, for Amelia Joe was a favorite in the village. David is the only member of the family who does not sit with the others; newly confirmed, he is assisting Father Frank, who happens to be in the village, at the mass for the dead. While the priest's voice drones on in English, followed by Great-uncle Wally with the Yup'ik translation, Adeline holds her little sister Lilly on her lap and tries to keep her quiet, but Lilly wriggles and squirms and occasionally breaks loose to run up the aisle of the crowded church to find someone else she knows.

Trying to concentrate on his duties as acolyte, David suddenly remembers when he took Great-grandmother Amelia some ducks last spring, and she promised that she would make him a seal-gut parka when he got his first seal. But she died before he could do that, and he knows that he will never have such a beautiful garment, because she is the last person in the village who still made them. In spite of her demonstrations at school, no one has the skill. It makes him very sad.

Walter Prescott races excitedly from room to room in the school with the big news: national television is sending a crew out from Anchorage to do a "Good

Morning America" sequence for the ABC morning program.

On the last day of September the *kass'aq* producer and crew arrive on a morning flight and check out the scene. The day is blustery and cold, and they decide to have everyone stand on the steps of the school, not the main entrance on the north but around on the south, out of the wind. The producer gets everybody arranged—the dance team in their matching *qaspeqs* in the middle, and some of the elders who have shown up in their best parkas down in front. When the crew is finally satisfied with the setup, they give it a couple of practice runs. Then, while the TV camera rolls, Walter Prescott shouts, "These are the students and teachers of Urrsukvaaq School in Chaputnguak, Alaska."

On cue David and Adeline and their brothers and sisters and all the kids of Chaputnguak wave and holler joyously to the whole USA somewhere out there beyond their village, "Good morning, America!"

EPILOGUE: HOW THIS BOOK CAME ABOUT

In the spring of 1976 Carolyn Meyer visited the village of Chefornak, the guest of Bernadine Larsen, a *kass'aq* married to a Yup'ik Eskimo. The two women had been corresponding, and their friendship-by-mail resulted in a decision to work on a book together about a subject that fascinated them both: life in Bernadine Larsen's village. In *Eskimos: Growing Up in a Changing Culture* they created a fictional village which they named Chaputnuak, the original name of Chefornak, and they peopled the village with fictional residents. Chaputnuak—which is how it was spelled then—was not meant to be exactly like Chefornak, but rather like many similar Yup'ik villages in the Yukon-Kuskokwim Delta. And the Koonuk family was a composite of many different people.

After the book was published in 1977, Carolyn and Bernie, caught up in their busy lives, gradually lost touch. But in the spring of 1994, Carolyn began to dream of writing another book, picking up where *Eskimos* had left off. She managed to track down Bernie, who had left the village, remarried, and eventually moved to the other side of the continent. They decided to revisit Chefornak, where Bernie's children still live, and to write a new book that would reflect the changes in the lives of the Yup'ik Eskimos.

This time the visit was in the fall. While Bernie played with her grandson, Carolyn camped out in a kindergarten classroom. She found a village that had grown a great deal in size, from 211 to 361, with a state-of-the-art school for all village children and computers and a satellite dish but still no plumbing in the houses and a concern with growing social problems.

Elders lament the loss of Yup'ik traditions. Young people yearn for a future that lets them live as Yup'iks while living the dream of a job and financial benefits. In some ways everything is different; in some ways nothing has changed. Perhaps, the author believes, the greatest change is in herself, in her maturing experience as a writer and her broader perceptions as a human being.

In a Different Light: Growing Up in a Yup'ik Eskimo Village picks up with the Koonuk family eighteen years later; Jim Koonuk, a high school senior in the earlier book, is now himself the father of school-age children. It is through David and Adeline and their brothers and sisters that the story of the Real People continues to unfold.

BIBLIOGRAPHY

Barker, James H. *Always Getting Ready: Yup'ik Eskimo Subsistence in Southwest Alaska.* Seattle: University of Washington Press, 1993.

Carey, Richard Adams. *Raven's Children: An Alaskan Culture at Twilight.* Boston: Houghton Mifflin, 1992.

Fienup-Riordan, Ann. *The Nelson Island Eskimo.* Anchorage: Alaska Pacific University Press, 1983.

Lenz, Mary, and James H. Barker. *Bethel: The First 100 Years.* Bethel, AK: A City of Bethel Centennial History Project, 1985.

Meyer, Carolyn. *Eskimos: Growing Up in a Changing Culture.* New York: McElderry/Atheneum, 1977.

Oswalt, Wendell H. *Bashful No Longer: An Alaskan Eskimo Ethnohistory, 1778–1988.* Norman: University of Oklahoma Press, 1980.

GLOSSARY OF YUP'IK WORDS

akutaq—dish made of berries, fat, sugar, and other ingredients
angun—man; literally "a device for catching food"
Calista—regional corporation of Alaska; literally "our thing"
camai—welcome
kalukaq—feast
kass'aq—white person
Mamterillermiut—early name of Bethel; literally "people of many fish caches"
mukluk—literally "large seal"; has come to be *kass'aq* word for sealskin boot
muqtuq—blubber
nakaciuq—village festival
qasgiq—men's communal house; steam bath house
qaspeq—cotton parka cover worn by women
qayaq—kayak; skin boat
teq'uq—urine
uluaq—woman's knife
uqiquq—seal party
yaaruin—story knife
yua—soul; literally "its person"
Yup'ik—literally "the Real People"

INDEX

A

Akutaq; see Glossary, 24, 103, 104, 113, 153
Alaska, 2, 13-18, 141-143
Alaska Native Land Claims Settlement Act, 142-143
Alaska Permanent Fund, 35-36
Alcohol and Drinking, 66, 70, 127, 135, 157
Alphabet, Yup'ik, 86-87
Anchorage, 12, 146-150
Arctic Ocean, 2, 13, 14, 133

B

Babies, rearing, 112, 115-117
Barge shipments, 6, 12, 23, 153-155
Baseball, 60,140
Basketball, 28-30
Basketmaking, 75, 77-79, 148
Beadwork, 81-82
Bering, Vitus, 16
Bering Sea, 11, 13, 15, 90
Berries, gathering, 27, 152-153
Bethel, 22, 38, 62, 63, 64, 85, 87, 89, 127, 132-135,143
Bingo, 36-37
Birth, 62, 143
Blackfish, 165-166
Bladder, seal, 55
Blubber, 100-101
Bootlegging, 66, 68
Bristol Bay, 118, 126, 127

C

Calista, 143
Canada, 14, 15
Caribou, 24
Christmas, 38-42
Chugach Mountains, 147
Cooking, 23-24, 99
Crime, 70, 135

D

Dancing, 56, 57-58

Death, 64-66, 70, 165-171
Denali National Park, 144
Dillingham, 123, 126
Diseases, 61, 62, 64-66, 67, 71
Dogsled team, 14, 45, 127
Driftwood, 150-151
Drugs, 69, 157
Drumming, 58
Ducks, hunting, 98-99

E

Eggs, gathering, 99, 107-108
English, use of, 20, 87, 160
Eskimo, 14-15, 85-88
Eskimo ice cream, 24, 103, 104, 113, 153
Eskimo yo-yo, 142

F

Fairbanks, 147
Fetal alcohol syndrome, 67, 69
Fish camp, 15, 51, 128
Football, 138, 140
Fourth of July, 135-142
Fox, 34, 35
Fur clothing, 42, 57, 81-82, 100-101
  Trading, 16
  Trapping, 33-35

G

Graduation, 117-119
Grass, gathering, 7, 77, 120, 166-168
Greens, gathering, 27, 51, 120-121

H

Health care, 61-66, 142
Herring, 123-126
Honey bucket, 6, 8, 65
Hunting, 15, 27, 55, 83, 90-99, 102-103, 111, 121, 121-123, 164, 165
Husband, role of, 50-51, 110-115

I

Ice fishing, 30, 31, 166

Indians, American, 14, 15
Intestine, seal, 74-76, 83, 101, 171
Inuits, 14-15, 85
Inupiats, 15
Ivory, 79-80

J

Juneau, 18

K

Kayak, 15, 82-83
Kodiak Island, 16
Kuskokwim River, 11-12, 15, 18, 49, 128
Language, Yup'ik, 16, 20, 85-88
Lemmings, 120-121, 169

M

Marriage, 48, 49, 110-115
Men's communal house, 50-52, 82, 138
Mink, 33-34
Missionaries, Christian, 18, 53, 54, 56, 86, 114, 115
  Moravian, 18, 54, 59, 80, 134
  Roman Catholic, 18, 54
  Russian Orthodox, 17, 54
Moose, 164
Moravians, 18, 54, 59, 80, 134
Mosquitoes, 144-145
Mount Edgecumbe, 22, 118
Mount McKinley, 144
Mukluks, 81-82
Muqtuq; see Glossary, 100-101
Musk ox, 34-35
Muskrat, 121-123

N

Naming, 53-54, 116
Nunivak Island, 35

P

Permafrost, 11, 13
Pilot bread, 10, 47, 58, 96, 102
Poaching, 79-80
Potlatch, 56-60

Ptarmigan, 80, 98, 107-108
Public watering point, 5-6, 65

Q

Qasgiq; see Glossary, 50-52, 82, 138
Qaspeq; see Glossary, 83-85

R

Raven, 49
Reindeer, 24
Remedies, traditional, 64
Roman Catholics, 18, 54
Russians, 15-17, 52, 54, 65, 81

S

Salmon, 126-130
Seal, spirit of, 55
Seal butchering, 100-102, 111-112
Seal hunting, 15, 27, 83, 90-98, 102-103, 111, 164, 165
Seal oil, 24, 101
Seal party, 88, 99-100, 103-105
Seal-gut parka, 74-76, 83, 101, 171
Sealskin, 42, 100-101
Seward, William H., 18
Sex, outside of marriage, 72-73, 115
Shamanism, 54, 55-56
Skin sewing, 42, 80-81, 82
Smelt, 31
Snow machines and
Snowmobiles, 7, 41, 42-44, 56, 66
Sod houses, 50- 52
Soul, 54-56, 80, 169
Southeastern Alaska, 11-12, 16
Spirit, 54-56, 116
Steam bath, 52-53
Storyknifing, 108-110
Storytelling, 47-50, 108-110, 122
String stories, 109, 110
Subsistence, 105-106
Suicide, 66, 70, 135
Summer solstice, 130-131

T

Thule Eskimos, 14-15
Tobacco; "chew", 70-71, 168
Tomcod, 30, 31-32
Tourists, 79, 144
Traders, 16, 79
Tundra, 2, 11, 89-90

U

Uluaq; see Glossary, 100
Uqiquq; see Glossary, 88, 99-100, 103, 105, 108
Urine, 75

V

VPSO, 36, 68, 161

W

Walrus, 79-80
Wedding, 113-115
Whale, 15, 165
Whitefish, 58
Wife, role of, 50-51, 110, 115
Willow, 71, 166, 168
Woman's knife, 100

Y

Yaaruin; see Glossary, 105-110
Yua; see Glossary, 54-56, 80, 169
Yukon River, 11-12
Yup'ik Eskimos, 12, 15, 28-30, 49, 69, 85